SISTER JO

SISTER JOSEPHINE

Joanna Traynor

BLOOMSBURY

My thanks to Sarah Kenny, Marsha Hunt,
and the Saga Group.

First published 1997

Copyright © 1997 by Joanna Traynor

The moral right of the author has been asserted

Bloomsbury Publishing Plc, 38 Soho Square, London W1V 5DF

A CIP catalogue record for this book is
available from the British Library

ISBN 0 7475 3377 6

10 9 8 7 6 5 4 3 2 1

Typeset by Hewer Text composition services, Edinburgh
Printed in Great Britain by Clays Ltd, St Ives plc

To Robbie

PART I

Chapter 1

The policewoman looked dead serious when she asked me.

'Are your mam and dad West Indians?' Softly she said it, like it was a secret.

I was scared. If I hadn't been scared I would have laughed me head off. Imagining me mum and dad with tomahawks and machetes, going pow-wow-wow with their hands across their mouths. I didn't know there was a difference between a West Indian and a Red one then. I was nine and a bit and brown.

'No. They're more like cowboys – like you,' I said, pointing to her white hand.

I knew why she was asking though. Coz of Butlin's. At Butlin's they made me be an Injun coz I was brown. I wanted to be a cowboy because Injuns were bad. They said I had to be an Injun or I couldn't play. Turned out the cowboys were more terrifying than the Injuns. I'm not keen on water but those cowboys terrified me so much I had to climb into the water fountain – one of them that's shaped like a wedding cake. Because I was stood right behind the roaring waterfalls, they couldn't lasso me. Then all of them, the cowboys *and* the Injuns, did loads of 'Yee-haa-ing' and 'Pow-wow-ing', all around the fountain.

'I didn't mean . . .' The policewoman trailed off into a sigh.

I was counting the swerves of the police car so I could tell when we were in Duchy Street. Our street. I couldn't see out of the windows. They were all steamed up. And it was raining. There were hundreds and thousands of little water blobs careering down the glass. And by Duchy Street, I was crying me eyes out.

The car juddered to a halt outside our house, one of many in a vast army of council houses marching for miles around. It was a big solid house and from the front, just three windows floating in a sea of dark-brown brick. When I got out of the car I noticed all the curtains were closed. They couldn't have all gone to bed. It wasn't past tea time.

The policewoman had me by the arm. She didn't want to hold my hand because I'd been naughty but she didn't want to drag me by the scruff either. The policeman driver stayed in his seat, his head bent over the steering-wheel. He looked like the hearse drivers outside St Bede's church. They always looked like that when they were waiting for a body to come out.

'Too small a garden to fanny about with a lawn,' my dad said.

He used it for flowerbeds and roses. The roses weren't out yet and the daffodils were in church in thick glass vases underneath the stations of the cross.

A chill pawed at my face. A cold wet slap.

I kept my head right down. The front door opened. The first thing I saw was my dad's feet in his slippers with all

4

the backs squashed down. The skin on his foot was shiny and pink like baby skin.

'Af'noon,' he said. 'What's the trouble 'ere then?'

'Er, Mr Milner?'

'Aye.'

'Errh, Mr Milner,' pushing me forwards towards him. 'Shoplifting,' as though she was introducing me. 'Oboe's. Won't be pressing charges. This time.'

'Get in.'

He said 'Get in' so quietly I looked up to convince myself he'd said it. He could have said it louder than that. The skin around his eyes was blue-red. Like stuff that you see at the butcher's with all the veins popping out. Looked dead sore. The whites of his eyes were like crazy paving in red. He was toppling like he might fall over. I wanted to hold him up. What was he playin' at? He wasn't acting like a proper dad. He didn't even go for me. I was kinda waitin' for it. Bein' polite. I thought the policewoman would wanna see that I was being dealt with but he just stood there dead dozy.

His mouth opened to speak and then closed again. His cheeks were all saggy. His bald head made it worse. I nearly choked on that. His saggy cheeks and bald head stuttering in the doorway. God, Dad!

'Get in, I said.'

I shot up the stairs. Crouched down on the landing, I carried on listening.

'You'll 'ave to excuse us, miss, for not askin' yer inside, only there's been a death in the family and it's . . . well, it's not the time, if yer know what I mean. Can I contact the station later on praps?'

I hoped it was Gary who was dead. I wanted his bike.

5

I heard his bedroom door open behind me.

''Snot you that's dead then.'

He grabbed the back of my dress and pulled me up – like I was the tail of a dead cat coz my dress was really soggy. He wiped his hand on his trousers in disgust.

'Look at yer. Just look at the state. Wait till me mam gets yer. Nickin' from Oboe's. Not bein' 'ere when your gran died. You've 'ad it.'

He bolted me into my bedroom on the end of his foot like I was a football. He often did that. Grabbed hold of me, positioned me and then bam! He shot the ball. I landed with my head buried into the wall.

'Hurt, did it? I hope so. Let's see if this hurts . . .'

He came in for a big long ear rub.

I caught my breath and screamed at the top of. I was shaking like mad. Full up of it all.

I heard her coming up the stairs. A slow shuffling. Certain steps on the creaky boards. In order. Silent. I pulled off my shoes and climbed into bed. I sat with my knees tucked up under my chin. Slobber. And much snot. I wanted kid talk. Soft talk. Maybe Granny dying was an opening. We'd never had a death before. Maybe like on telly, when someone dies and everyone starts being nice. The grown-ups. Dad didn't hit me. Maybe.

'What's the yarlin' for?'

She was holding on to the door handle, her body partly shielded by the door. Her face full on. She looked tired, haggard. She was quite old compared to other mums. Over fifty at least. Too old and orange to be my real mum anyway. Her hair was greying at the sides a little but mostly it was orange, like her freckles, which were all over. Most of her freckles were like dot-to-dot but in some places, like on her

6

arms, there were so many of them, they joined up and if I looked really quickly, open eye-shut eye, her arm looked nearly brown like mine. Especially in the summer.

She was small with loads of bulk in the belly. Her belly filled the pockets of her pinny so that when she had something inside them, she looked deformed. I searched the belly for the outline of the black leather strap. The belly looked smooth.

'It was 'im.'

'It was 'im!' she snarled. 'It's always 'im, int it, eh? Well, yer can't blame 'im for today's shenanigans, young lady. He was 'ere when your gran died . . . not out cavortin' with the devil.'

My mum's face was nearly as wrinkled as Gran's. I figured she'd be next. It wouldn't be a day too soon. Her stockings were orange too. They were usually rolled down to her ankles so it looked like she had quoits on. But they weren't now. This was a sign that she was going out.

'We're goin' out. Martin's stayin' 'ere and 'e's been given his orders not to let you downstairs, not for anything. Now then, I suggest you kneel down and say some prayers. Go on! On your knees and say your prayers.'

I didn't want to move. I joined my hands together, sat in the bed and closed my eyes, hoping and praying that the gesture was enough.

The scream that followed was one of those that nearly breaks the camel's back. If I didn't move now I'd be dragged out of the bed and battered. But before I could, she was on me. She lunged forward, grabbed me by me arm and pulled me from the blankets. My knee banged against the bed railing hitting my funny bone. I yelled out in agony, falling on the floor as a bag of bones. Jangling.

'Now say 'em.'

Thank God for prayers. If there hadn't been prayers there'd have been something much worse. With all her heavy breathing and my snuffles it didn't feel very prayer-like though. Not proper prayer.

'Matthew, Mark, Luke and John.'

I had my head down but I couldn't resist sneaking a look for a saint on the bedposts. My eyeballs rolled around scanning each corner of the bed. It's funny coz I thought I'd get a crack round the earhole if I got caught doing that. Looking for the saints.

'Bless this bed that I lay on. And if I die before I wake, I pray the Lord my soul do take. God bless Mum and Dad and Grandma and Gary and Martin and all the starving people in Africa. Help me to be a better person and help me work well at school. Amen.'

'Now get in bed and stay there.'

After a few minutes I heard Gary come out of his room. He put his head around the door and spat a huge sac of gob on to the bed. It landed on the blanket just missing me. I retched. I took my dress off and with the soggy bits, I rubbed the spit into the blanket.

Within minutes, I heard the front door slam and then footsteps down the path. I heard the van titter to a start. Titter titter, brum and they were gone.

Chapter 2

Then I heard Boylie.

'Jos-eeeee, Jos-seeee!'

I parted the curtains to see him. He was leaning against the gate on his bicycle. *Still* wearing his balaclava. Coz of that balaclava Oboe couldn't be sure it was him. And he couldn't catch him to find out coz as soon Boylie realised that I'd been caught red-handed he was off on his bike, ringing his bell and whistling his little head off. I opened the window and shouted down to him.

'Me grandma's dead.'

'I know.'

I closed the curtains and left him swinging on the gate. He was dying to know more. What did she look like? Were her eyes still in? Where was the body? Was I gonna tell on him?

Where *was* the body?

Above the curtains there was a new pelmet that me dad put in as a shelf for all the round-the-world dolls. Each doll was about four inches high and just stood there. They didn't do anything. Their arms didn't even move. I didn't like dolls anyway. Gran and Aunty Beth bought the dolls for me because they said I was collecting them. But I wasn't. *They* were. There was a Welsh doll, a Scottish one, a soldier from outside Buckingham Palace with a big black hat on. There was an Eskimo in a white coat with a furry hood and there was a funny man with short trousers and a bib on from Germany. My favourite was the Red Indian. She stood straight and proud and serious. Not like me snivelling in the fountain. She had a bow-and-arrow set and a short suede dress, jagged at the edges. I wanted to be her. With long straight hair. I wanted to put an arrow straight through Gary's head and watch it come out the other side.

I was naked. I put my frock, which was all but demolished, under the bed. I wanted it to disappear. Under the bed seemed the best way to make it do this. One day it would be found. There were no clean nighties in the drawer. They were all downstairs in the washing basket pretending to be waiting for an iron. There were clothes at the bottom of that basket that waited and waited. There were skirts with pleats in and thick orange curtains that weren't needed till wintertime. Every year, they weren't needed till wintertime. Forbidden to go downstairs, I slid inside the sheets, damp. Crumbs, remnants of a custard-cream binge, lodged inside the crack of me bottom. Sleep was unimaginable.

The bubbles came.

The first time I saw the bubbles I was lying in bed old enough to know that bubbles didn't just come out of thin air. I was old enough to study the difference between day and night. I studied shapes in the dark to identify each one as I knew it by light.

Then the bubbles came. The bubbles mounted the shapes.

10

Then exploded into mini-blizzards. Bubbles with white edging. All across my eyes.

The bogy man was blowing the bubbles.

I screamed the place down.

My mum came and took me to her bed. That was the first and last time she did that. Next time the bubbles came, I had to put up with them.

I was wondering where the body was and the bubbles were back. It was just getting dark. I leant forward in the bed to look at myself in the mirror. The princess's mirror, I called it. The shape of my hair reminded me of the doll with the red coat on from Buckingham Palace.

'Josie . . . Josie . . . Come downstairs! I'm making chips.'

''M not allowed.'

'I said so.'

'I can't.'

'Why?'

'I haven't got a nighty.'

'I'll bring one up for yer.'

Martin was the opposite to Gary. He was all right. Not hard. Mind, he was grown-up nearly. He worked in a casino and went to the pub. My dad couldn't stand that. He had high hopes for Martin. Thought he'd be a priest. Was such a dedicated altar boy. Always round at the church. Always helping Father Brady.

He stopped going. Stopped dressing up in altar-boy clothes. Now he wore long trousers with great wide flares that covered his feet. And glasses. His hair was blond and rimmed with baby curls and he was dead spotty.

''Ere it is then.' He waited at the door – waited for me to put it on.

'Where's me nighty?' He was dangling one of his shirts.

'The washin' on the pulley's still wet. You'll 'ave to make do with that. Well, go on then, put it on.'

'Well, *you* go on then.'

'You're not shy, are yer? I used to bath yer, remember. You're still only a little girl, yer know.'

'No I'm not.' I reached over for the shirt and put it on still sat in bed.

'C'mon then.' He held out his hand.

When we reached the landing, we both paused and looked at the door to Gran's room.

'Is she in there?'

'Gran? . . . No, stupid. She's at the hospital.'

I looked at the door again. I figured she was in purgatory. Nowhere near the hospital.

The smell of dripping snarled when the dining-room door opened. To the kitchen. Martin headed straight for the cooker and stabbed at the dripping with a spatula to make it melt faster. I could just make out the 'RTIN' of his name engraved in the fat. He smashed at this bit first. He didn't think I'd seen. The potatoes were chipped and ready to go as soon as the fat had melted. Each chip was about the size of a fish finger.

'Big chips,' I said.

I watched until the chips were brown. I offered to butter the mountain of bread that he took from the bread bin but he refused and said he'd do it his way. 'His way' was spreading half-inch-thick layers of Stork margarine on each slice, slice after slice. No ceremony. Like he was brick-laying.

I tiptoed towards the sink navigating the mini-puddles

12

that were forming on terracotta tiles. I looked up to the wooden pulley. It was overloaded with wet clothes. It made the room dark and cloggy. Smoke from the chip pan was curling round the sheets.

'Somebody'll be moanin' their bed stinks o' chips,' I said.

He never said anything. Never looked. Intent on his chips. Concentration. I just wanted to feel part of it.

I leant against the sink. I used to stand in that sink and be washed like a pan when I was really little. Sometimes through the window I saw kids staring at me from the field at the bottom of the yard. I took some plates and forks from the draining board and put them on the side next to the cooker. From one of the half-height cupboards painted undercoat-sky blue I reached in for the tin of salt, tomato sauce and a jar of pickled-onion vinegar that was still left over from Christmas. Martin arranged the plates on top of the washing machine. It was a fat washing machine with a lid on top and a mangle that was stuck on so tight it had to stay up all the time. He moved the wooden clothes tongs to make way for the plates. One tong nearly caught fire and I jumped to save it catching, throwing it in the sink to stop it smoking. He glanced a thank you.

The shirt was so wide it wouldn't rest easy on my shoulders. I had to keep holding it all together. It gave me something to fiddle with when I couldn't find anything else to do or say. When the chips were out and the pan turned off, Martin picked up his plate and bread and headed off like a waiter. I picked up my own plate and followed him out of the kitchen through the dining room and into the front room. I bent down to put my plate on the coffee table and the shirt fell away from

13

my shoulders to the ground. I let go of the plate too quickly trying to cover myself. The chips slid off. I was standing there in the glare of him. He didn't linger with his stare. He started pulling all the black bits off me chips. And then I remembered all those bath times he was on about.

When the meal was done I cleaned up. I even put the pan of hot dripping back in the oven and although it swayed a lot in its flat and wide container I didn't panic or spill any. Then I headed off back up the stairs. I shouted 'Nye Gobless' but he called me back.

'Where yer goin'? Come in and watch the telly. *Randall and Hopkirk*'s on.'

'They'll be back soon.'

'No they won't. They've gone visitin' to tell everyone about Gran. They won't be back for ages yet. Come on. It's me that'll get into trouble, not you.'

I didn't want to. I couldn't enjoy the telly listening out for the van all the time but I didn't want to seem ungrateful. I didn't want to believe in ghosts. Not that night. I sat on the couch like a stranger at a party.

The Flake advert came on and I asked him if he wanted a cup of tea. He didn't answer. I didn't know whether he heard me or not. I was a bit scared of him. Not because he was dangerous or anything, but because I didn't really know him that well. I hadn't spent much time alone with him so I had no way of knowing what he was thinking, what he liked or didn't like. What he might do next. What he might say. I tried again and this time he did reply. He said, 'No.'

I leant forward to play with my toes. I still kept me eyes on the telly. I wasn't watching it though. I was thinking about how to get back upstairs. All the times I was sent to bed early, I devised plots and sub-plots on how to get downstairs. And now, I was plotting to get back up there again.

He turned to look at me. I didn't look back at him but I could see from the corner of me eye that he was looking and still looking. I bored a hole in the telly with my stare. I didn't know why but I was rigid.

I threw some chit-chat into the silence to fill the hollow a bit.

'S'pose you'll be movin' into Gran's room now. You'll 'ave your own room and not 'ave to put up with our Gary any more.'

'Yep! That's the plan. I'll start paintin' soon as they've finished mournin'.'

'When's that?'

'When's what?'

'When do they finish mournin'?'

'Dunno. After the funeral, I s'pose. Probably the week after. Can't start too soon, anyroads. Wouldn't be right.'

'Bet yer can't wait.'

'Oh, I can wait. I gotta buy all the paint. It'll take me two weeks' wages to get all that sorted, no doubt.'

'I wish I could paint me own room.'

'Never mind about paintin'. Come over 'ere.'

I jerked.

'Why?'

'Coz I want yer to.'

'What for?'

'Coz I want yer to. I just said, didn't I? Come 'ere!'

I moved along the couch towards him.

'Not there. Come 'ere and stand in front of me.'

'Why?'

'Coz I wanna tell yer a secret.'

'Yer can tell me 'ere.'

'I don't want to.'

He was getting impatient. I didn't want to start a row so I got up off the couch and stood in front of him. He pulled me closer and he opened his legs wide enough to hold my legs inside them. He pushed the inside of his knees against my thighs and at the same time held both my hands. Not the palms of my hands, more the wrists. It was quite comfy. I felt close to him. It was odd being close to anyone but I liked Martin.

'What's the secret then?'

'You're gonna be sharing a bedroom.'

'Who with?'

He let go of one of my wrists. My shirt dropped off one of my shoulders and he pulled it back up to my neck.

'A new girl.'

Pictures of all the girls in my class swam through my brain.

'What new girl?'

'From St Barny's.'

He didn't take control of my wrist again. Instead he stroked the side of my leg, the way I stroked the fluffy dog that was sat on my dressing table. Up and down. Up and down.

St Barny's was the children's home next to Nazareth

16

House where I came from. If you weren't fostered or adopted from Nazareth House you graduated to St Barny's.

'How d'yer know?'

I scratched my leg where he was stroking me. His touch was tickling me. A down-to-earth scratch. He stroked me harder.

'I heard.'

He was enjoying his power. He had a grin from ear to ear. I was pleased. I wanted a sister. I needed as much protection from Gary as I could get.

'How old is she then?'

'I dunno.'

His hands, both hands, were now holding the backs of my legs. My thighs. They slid higher and higher. He was holding my bum, moving his hands round and round. It was still comfy. I knew he was being rude. I acted like nothing was wrong. I liked the feel of his hands. They were warm and soft. They felt safe.

'Well, will she be older than me or what?'

'Oh yeah, she's older than you. Much older. Older than Gary. Now that's it. I'm not sayin' any more. I shouldn't've said anythin'. When you find out proper, you pretend you didn't know, right?'

'Right.'

If she was older than Gary that meant she was a teenager. That'd kill him.

'And you don't tell anybody about tonight. About the chips or anything, right?'

'Right.' I knew by 'anything', he meant 'everything'.

'Go on then. You'd better get up 'em. They'll be 'ome soon.'

I pulled at my shirt to assemble the mass in front of me

17

and walked to the door. Martin sat biting his fingernails staring at the television. He didn't look at me again.

'Nye Gobless.'

'Nye Gobless.'

Chapter 3

Some Saturday. Gary was out playing football. Dad working. Mum was in town. Martin. Normally he went to his casino friend's house in town on Saturday. I got to work on the stairs first. Before changing my bed. The handbrush was battered. It stroked the fluff backwards and then forwards again. Elbow grease made clouds of it. Martin came up the stairs behind me. Ran his hands up my legs. I jumped. He pushed past me, took the brush from my hand and pulled me up the stairs. I didn't fall into his hands easily but I didn't put up much of a struggle either. We went to my bedroom.

He crouched down to examine me. I held my dress like a can-can girl and inspected his golden crown in the princess's mirror. I dreamed each curl a single golden coin full of chocolate. I moved where he wanted me to move and said nothing. His probing fingers didn't hurt me. They crept over and under me. Like visitors. When he was finished he was breathing heavy. He got up and walked out.

Later on, he found me on the landing looking for sheets in the airing cupboard. He held my arm firmly, stopping the search. His face was blackened with darkness. I couldn't see any cheery welcome. My spotty friendly brother.

'Don't tell anybody at school. Don't breathe a word of it to anyone – anywhere. You know where you'll go if you do, don't yer?'

I wanted to think he was a bastard but he still gave me the crackling off his roast pork. He never raised his voice. He never beat me up. He kept Gary off me. Made him surrender. Writhe. Squirm. Beg on his knees for forgiveness. I only had to say the word. When he was home.

Gary was back with his friend Ginge, Boylie's brother. They were restless and high-spirited. Nearly thirteen, they were too old to be playing in dens and the like but too young for day-long excursions to town. They were in the back yard practising knots with bits of rope. Ginge made a sort of pulley device which opened the doors to the shed and toilet automatically, the rope threaded through the two door handles. They wanted to make use of it. As I shut the gate I sensed trouble.

''Ere, Josie, come here!'

'No.'

'Oh go on. We wanna try somethin'.'

'What?'

'Look at this.'

Ginge pulled on the ropes doin' the trick.

'Big deal.'

'No. That's not all. Come 'ere and 'old the ropes for us.'

'What for?'

'Come 'ere and we'll show yer.'

I quite fancied having a go at pulling on the ropes.

'Right, Ginge. You get 'old of her an' I'll get the rope sorted. Pin 'er against the wall.'

I fought as well as I could. They were careful not to let my head bang against the concrete path. They tied my feet to the door handles. My legs akimbo. Showing my knickers. That was the upsetting thing but they didn't even mention my knickers. They were obsessed with the invention. They made me part of the pulley. I was like a swing bridge. My body tilted with the pull, one leg coming out as the toilet door opened and vice versa. In-out-in-out. It only worked a couple of times then something went wrong. They were bored with it. They couldn't be bothered making it work again. Gary started tickling my ribs which made me laugh hard and loud at first. Then drained me. Tortured me. The boys were bent over double holding their ribs in agony, laughing.

'You bastards, you bloody bastards . . .'

'Watch your language. You know what happens to little girls who swear, don't yer?'

Gary came back from the kitchen with a bottle of washing-up liquid and set about squeezing the nozzle between my lips. I couldn't keep my lips tight together for long and I let out one long scream which allowed him to fill my mouth with New! Sunlight Washing-Up Liquid.

Martin heard the screaming. He made Ginge untie the ropes and whisked Gary off into the house. Ginge did a quick one over the back fence and I went to the kitchen to rinse my mouth out. From the sink I could see Gary pinned to the kitchen floor, Martin's legs over his arms and their heads only inches apart. Martin spat in his face. I saw the spit running down his nose and into his eyes. He kept spitting, one blob after another. Silent and intense. Gary begged for forgiveness. Martin slapped him. Cheek after cheek. Slap. Slap. Slap. Slap.

'I'm sorry, I'm sorry . . . stop, please stop.'

Martin was quiet. Usually he had a go, shouting and berating, but he was dead quiet. Somat was different about this. Gary sensed it too. Martin started bouncing his head against the terracotta tiles. Then a piercing scream. I jumped between them. I thought he was gonna kill him. For me. As a sort of payment. I didn't care about Gary one bit. But I knew that Mum'd go mad if she came home and he was dead. She'd do her nut. That was why I saved him.

Chapter 4

Some Sunday. Wilcox was late. She finally drew up outside the house in a mini. Like a chauffeur she opened up the passenger door to free her companion, Bernadette. Before walking the path, Bernadette paused at the gate to get a good look at the house, allowing me and Gary a good look at her. She was a real-life version of the Red Indian doll that sat on the pelmet in my bedroom. A brown girl with a long black plait that curved around her neck and hung down the front of her body. At the bottom of the plait there was a red ribbon. I craned my neck to see if she had a set of bow and arrows over her shoulder.

They were all being posh and polite in the hallway and then the front-room door opened and in she walked. Her dress, wild red with toggling white buttons, had a pleated skirt that fell just above the knee. She had on white patent shoes that were for ladies. Her black mane shone in achievement, its patterned length roped with strength. Her skin warm coffee, milky rich. A goddess. Bernadette breathed smiles of small white crystal sugar lumps. Joy.

I did my hellos with shy smiles, covering my mouth with my hand, to conceal my ecstasy.

Gary never even said hello.

Wilcox and Bernadette sat together on the couch, both with legs politely crossed, each balancing a small plate of two jam tarts. The tarts were on the plate for some time. They eyed them with suspicion. They were jam tarts all right but the jam wasn't normal red jam. It was greengage jam. No one likes green jam. I watched them on the couch balancing the plates, not looking at the tarts. It was like watching amateur explorers at a cannibal's tea party.

'I don't like jam,' whinged Bernadette.

'Oh don't yer! Well, I hope you're not the fussy sort, else you'll find yerself in a spot o' bother in this house, I'm afraid.'

'Praps she doesn't like green jam,' I piped up, trying to help her out.

'Well, I must say,' said Wilcox, taking the escape route for herself, 'I'm not too fond of green jam myself. I think I'll save my appetite. It's not such a long drive after here.'

Both plates hit the coffee table in a dance.

The three adults left the room to talk privately leaving us three in a hangar of silence. Bernadette was trying us out. If she liked us she'd be part of the family. If she didn't she'd go back to where she came from, Gary said.

Wilcox worked for Canon Doherty. He was Head of St Barnabas's Rescue. He was 'The Very Reverend' Canon Doherty. Always struck me as a bit uncreative, that title, but that's what they called him. His bellowing Irish chants got everyone on the go. Giving money, genuflections, signs of the cross and undivided attention. He didn't come much. Too busy rescuing. I was glad that I'd been rescued from Nazareth House. But I wanted to know where they got

24

me from. Where before Nazareth House? I couldn't ask. I thought it might sound ungrateful if I did.

Back came the adults and out went Gary and Bernadette. Bernadette, weighed down with bags and worry, was sent to the bedroom to unpack. Gary was sulking. He didn't even say goodbye to Mrs Wilcox. He just slammed the front door and ran down the path. Crying, I bet.

Wilcox was killing two birds with one stone. The three adults sat in front of me, Mrs Wilcox in charge. My mum and dad always looked nervous on these occasions. I could hear them thinking. Willing me to say the right thing.

Mrs Wilcox started: 'Whilst I was here for Bernadette, I thought we could do your report at the same time. Now then, how are things generally?'

Wilcox was getting on for being elderly. I was surprised she could drive because most women didn't and any that did didn't look like her. She had a big head and was all eyes. She wore too much orange lipstick on very big protruding lips. A purple rinse would have looked smashing on her, had she been a dinner lady. She had very very long eyelashes and myxomatosis eyes. Or it could have been her glasses that made her eyes look like that. She'd done away with her eyebrows completely in favour of hand-drawn, chocolate-coloured semi-circles. She looked about as sincere and down to earth as Danny La Rue.

'And school, how's school?'

'And do you have any problems you'd like to talk about?'

'So. All's well then?'

And *so* endeth the session. Wilcox got all the right answers to all the wrong questions. She mentioned there

25

being a little something to help with the housekeeping like we were in for kennelling.

I kept myself awake waiting for Bernadette to come to bed. She lifted her petticoat over her head, struggling a bit. I couldn't believe what was under that petticoat. Great white solid lumps shaped like shuttlecocks.

'What yer lookin' at?'

'Them.'

'Well, what about 'em?'

'What are they?'

'They're knockers, tits. What d'yer think they are?'

'What they for?'

'God, are you stupid or are you stupid? They're tits. It's my bust – breasts. Haven't yer seen a pair o' tits before?'

'No, I 'aven't. What's that for? To hide 'em?'

'It's a bra, divvy.'

She stood her gigantic nipple-suckers in front of me to give me a really good look. I shrank back. I was nearly in tears. It was like being assaulted.

'They're massive. They're horrible.'

'Well, you'll get 'em too. Yours'll be big an' all.'

Bernadette bent down to pick up the nightdress she'd laid out on the bottom bunk bed.

'No, I won't.'

'Course you will, stupid. All girls get 'em.'

'Mum 'asn't got 'em. She wears a vest like me.'

'Well, hers are all gone now, coz she's old. When you're old they go down like a balloon after a party.'

'Well, I'm not 'avin' 'em.'

I thought about all the women I knew. Mrs Marley at school. Well, yes, she did have lumps there but she was

26

fat. I always thought that the bumps were fat. Jennifer Joyce didn't have bumps, did she? I made a mental note to check her out.

I was getting used to such surprises. For instance, when I was learning to sew. My mum gave me a sewing set for Christmas. In it there were several pink-and-blue handkerchiefs with pictures of flowers and pretty maids on. The idea was to sew over the pictures, like tracing but with a needle and cotton. I started every handkerchief but I never finished one. The grubby pink-and-blue squares were abandoned all over the house. I used one to grease my pogo-stick. Anyway, I still had an ample supply of cotton and one big needle left. I set about looking for things to mend, things with holes in. I tore through the clean-washing basket determined to find a project. And then I came across Dad's underpants. Mature enough to sew, I felt mature enough not to have to wrench the inevitable glory from my mum and dad when they realised for themselves what a dab hand I was with a needle and thread. So I waited.

The following Sunday morning before church, I could hear him shouting and foot-stamping round the bathroom. That wasn't unusual. Then I heard doors banging and drawers being pulled out of the dressers and landing on the floor. Me mum rushed up to the rescue. When she came back down she took me aside.

'Never, not ever, do you touch your father's underpants again.'

I wasn't told why. I was supposed to work that one out for myself. I worked out that men were too lazy to pull down their underpants to go to the toilet and so they had to have a special hole to wee through.

Watching nappy changes of baby boys gave me some

27

insight into the willy wombat. It never occurred to me that the wombat grew bigger. I don't know why. It just didn't occur to me. It was my dad once again who suffered at the hands of my enlightenment. He often worked a nightshift at the Lecky, and one afternoon I was asked to go and wake him up. Carefully, with a mug of ritual tea in my left hand, I mounted the stairs. I heard his snores before I even reached halfway. Once in the room, the smell of ageing socks and slept-in blankets reeked around me. He lay flat on his back with his mouth wide open to form the letter 'O'. The room in semi-darkness reminded me of an animal's pit at the zoo. I shouted 'Dad' at him several times but the snores continued. He ground his teeth for a couple of seconds and again went back to snores.

A good shake was in order so I set about him. With the mug of steaming tea still in my left hand, I shook him with my right. I went straight for the middle of his body and found a rod to take hold of. I yanked the rod from side to side, up and down.

'Dad! Dad! Wake up now! Cup o' tea, Dad!'

He flew up the bed. Scalding tea lashed his balding head. He screamed at me really wild. Like that animal.

'Get out! Get out! Get out!' I was gone before the second 'Get Out!' had got out.

My mum later told me only ever to wake him up by shaking his shoulder. Nothing else. Just his shoulder.

Martin's was the first grown one I came face to face with. And it was face to face. Long hard pink with blue veins all around the top. Knobbly a bit. I couldn't work out how he hid it away when he was walking around. How did he bend it in so it didn't stick out of his trousers like a handle?

Bernadette's bust was just another bit of tackle to contend with. Bodies bulged and busted out all over the place. Willy wombats I already decided needed closer examination. What I always thought of as a worm somehow turned into a rod. The two little pink nibs of skin that pimpled my chest were going to grow into great big purple suckers on mountain slopes of fat sticking out further than my belly. Horrid!

'It's not because we're brown, is it?' I asked.

'What's not?'

'Them lumps on your chest.'

'No, stupid. Everybody . . . well, every woman gets 'em. Some get biguns and some don't. Yours'll be massive.'

'Oh shut yer gob, you. You're just sayin' that coz yours are. I 'ope yours get bigger.'

'So do I. Men like big tits.'

'Me dad doesn't. Look at me mum's. Eh, why is it you're brown and I'm brown and we've both been rescued and on telly I see pictures of starving brown babies in Africa and well . . . why do brown people always need rescuing?'

'Coz people don't like brown people.'

'Well, me mum and dad do, else we wouldn't be here. Who's your real mum and dad? Where are they?'

'I don't know. Shut up and go to sleep.'

'Maybe we're *real* sisters.'

'We're not, now shut up, will yer.'

The day after Bernadette came Gary had his head shaved.

'Skin'eads hate Pakis, wogs and trogs, greasers, hippies and mods but . . . especially Pakis.'

He managed to convince Mum to buy him, out of the catalogue, a crombie jacket and two Ben Sherman shirts.

29

His uniform. He wore two-tone trousers that looked green or blue depending on where you stood. I spent many an hour dubbing his monkey boots to a purple cherry. He sang songs like, '1, 2, 3, 4, knock a Paki off the wall. 6, 7, 8 9 10 . . . Never let him up again.'

Mum thought it was the fashion. She was pleased he didn't have long hair like the hippies on the telly running round at festivals with no clothes on. Short hair was more respectable. 'Oooh, look at 'im. He looks like a proper little soldier.' He looked as though he was waiting for a big cricket bat to come and knock his little block off.

He was a soldier in the lower ranks of an army of thugs. The Ridgehill Skinheads. Their clomping great bovver boots marched the streets of the estate singing songs of hate in new deep voices that still smacked of childhood. We were nignogs or wogs. I couldn't understand why all these boys hated us so much just because we were nignogs. After all, we were the only ones for miles around and . . . well . . . with there being so many of *them*, it seemed like overkill to say the least.

'Feel that.'

Gary showing me his steel toe-cap.

'Yeah?'

Me puzzled.

'AG . . . AGR . . . AGRO Agro,' he sang, knocking me flying on the 'Agro'.

I tried hard to make life up to Bernadette, to make her feel at home. But she was irritated by me. She didn't want me to see her being shamed by Gary. She insulated herself. And he laid right into her.

Chapter 5

Then Boylie started.

'Bet yer don't know where babies come from?'

When he told me I knocked him out. It was too much.

It was a miserable afternoon. The rain had stopped but it was nearly time to go in, so playing anything that involved leaving the street was out of the question. We were sat on the kerb talking, running sticks through sticky wet black stones lodged in the tarmac.

'Well, I know you don't find 'em under a bush.'

'Well, where do they come from then?'

'*I* don't know, do I?'

'D'yer want me to tell yer?'

'Why? Is it a secret or somat?'

'No, 'snot a secret but it's rude.'

'Rude? What's rude about babies?'

'Where they come from, stupid.'

'Oh come on, Boylie, pack it in. Get it out, whatever it is. You're makin' me 'ead ache.'

Boylie bent his head right down between his knees and dropped his voice to a whisper.

'When they want a baby, the man puts his willy inside

the woman's thingy and then a baby grows inside the woman's belly.'

That was it. No machines. No hospitals, doctors or cabinets full of drugs. No journeys on buses to collect them from a shop. That was it. I didn't believe him.

The wee-hole was all I knew about then (not including the poo-hole) and so that was the only 'thingy' that Boylie could have meant. Boylie was trying to tell me that men put their willy wombats, worms or rods, inside women's wee-holes. And anyway, how could a baby grow inside a stomach? There wasn't enough room.

I didn't respond immediately. I thought about all the impossibilities, one by one, and then turned on him.

'You're a liar, Boylie Bum.'

'No, I'm not.'

'Yes, you are.'

'Am not. Me mum told me.'

'Well your mum's a liar then as well.'

'Don't you call MY MUM a liar!'

'Well, she is. All you Proddy dogs are liars!'

With that Boylie grabbed hold of my hair and dragged me up from the kerb. My hair was that thick it didn't hurt. Hair-pulling never hurt me. It didn't half hurt the other kids though. I moved my head along with him pretending it was really hurting me. He thought I was in agony. With one quick yank I got myself out of his grip and elbowed him in the stomach. He jerked in pain and bent over to hug himself. With his defences down I grabbed hold of his hair, pulled it and then used it as a rope to throw him across the pavement. My hand let go too quickly but I managed to grab hold of his jumper and like our Gary I positioned my foot on his backside and then kicked him like a football towards the lamp post. It was a great goal. His head hit the lamp post bang on. He was knocked right out.

It was at school when all the pieces of everybody's body fell into place.

After assembly one morning, all the young kids filed out in crooked lines to their classrooms. Us, the fourth years, were told to stay put. There was an announcement for our ears only. The class muttered and mumbled. Mr Dowd – with just one finger slightly raised – brought the hall to silence.

This morning he was not smiling. If he did smile he smiled appropriately. If he saw a staff member in the corridor he smiled. Or on first seeing the face of a parent he *might* smile. It would come on like a light and go off again. This morning he was not smiling. He looked the way he looked when he told us that poor old Smudger had drowned in the canal. We were all looking around to see if anybody was missing. Then he started.

'Children, good morning.'

'Good – mor – ning – Mr – Dowd.'

'Now today, children, you are to be introduced to a new form of education, sex education.'

Silence.

'This afternoon, you will be given lessons regarding sex education which you will find useful and important later in life. This school has been chosen as one of the few in the country to offer this type of help to children as young as yourselves and it is hoped that you will understand and appreciate the seriousness of the subject. Now at one-thirty, after lunch, we want you all to congregate in class three. We ask you not to tell the other

33

children about this because they will be far too young to understand.

'Do you understand?'

'YES – MR – DOWD.'

'Any questions?'

Pause.

'Sir?'

'Yes, Stirrup?'

'Will we 'ave to do anythin'?'

The class was tittering.

'No, Stirrup, you won't have to *do* anything. Now, any more questions?'

'Sir, I was wondering . . . well . . . what is . . . sex education, I mean . . . what's sex, sir?'

After the question was out, all eyes turned to Dowdy. We never said 'sex'. It was one of those words that sat in the mind. Unused . . . known to be rude but useless. It wasn't a swear word. You couldn't call someone a 'sex'. Dowdy was going to talk to us about sex. He was wrestling with his tie and riding on the balls of his feet.

'Well, you'll find out all about that this afternoon, won't you? Now then, file out of the hall in silence and remember what I said about the rest of the children in the school. Keep this information to YOURSELVES.'

A whole afternoon was being given over to sex. The morning lessons were model. The milk bottles were collected in an orderly fashion by a number of volunteers. The spare milk was shared out to those who wanted it without one squeak of protest. Even from Micky Green who always insisted he was so poor he had to have all the spare milk to help him build his muscles up. Several boys jumped up to clean the blackboard between lessons until one boy finally got on with it. We weren't risking a thing.

We marched into class three and into the darkness. The mystery had begun. There was a film projector focused on a white canvas screen, a blank square light showing the area where the pictures would come up. We noticed it was the great big reel, not the carousel that just did photos but bigger. The reel meant moving pictures and we all got excited thinking there'd be live human beings doing sex on the classroom wall. There were no rabbit silhouettes from Stirrup in the vacant square of light, no screeching like before the wildlife slides at the end of every summer term. We sat really quietly. The air was full of anxious teachers. In the end one teacher, Miss Barlow, who couldn't stand the atmosphere any longer, ordered us to make a noise.

She began the session. She was oldish with a King Richard hairstyle. Her head was triangular, fat at the back and pointed at the face. Her wide mouth zipped from each side of each cheek to join in a 'V' at the lips. Everything about her had shape and regularity. We were scared of her. The staff were scared of her, especially the young ones. I could tell she didn't want to give the session. I saw a couple of the other teachers laughing at her. Dowdy must have made her do it.

'Right, children,' she started, hiding behind the film projector.

'Today we are going to see two films. The first is called *Growing Up* and then you will see another film entitled *Where Do Babies Come From?*.'

'Miss, can we see *Where Do Babies Come From?* first?'

'Shut up, Stirrup. Now before we start, does anybody want to go to the toilet?'

35

No response had the film reels noisily tracking their way around to the beginning of *Growing Up*.

There she was. A fattish-looking whale of a woman, white, save for some rouge on her cheeks, standing naked. It was only an illustration but a naked woman nevertheless. All the girls cringed. The boys sniggered. The inflated balloons were there for all to see. I hated it. Thank God Boylie wasn't there. And there were the hairs. Under the arms and on her thrupenny bit. Her arms and legs were all fat at the top and her face – she didn't look chuffed. All the girls were looking at each other, a bit scared. I felt sick. Then came the labels. Breasts. Pubic Hair. Nipples. Facial Hair. Then the skin became see-through and there were more pictures, this time of eggs and tunnels and more labels. Mammary Gland. Ovary. Vagina. There were little eggs floating down the tunnels one after the other and then breaking up. Uterus. Cervix. Canal. I thought of Smudger again when they went on about the canal. The girls were quieter than silent. Light relief was on its way. Up came the Man. Covered in hairs. Head to foot, he was covered in hairs. And there was his willy wombat about the size of a rocket lolly upside down. Behind it were some balls. Saggy and silly. Up came the labels. Scrotum. Penis. Pubic Hair. The girls roared. The film went on and on about the insides of bodies but we weren't really interested in the insides. Our appetites were satisfied.

'Any questions?'

Stirrup had to start. He wanted to know the word, the proper word, for the girl's thrupenny bit.

'Miss, what's it called, you know, the part of the woman where, you know, where she goes to the toilet?'

'That part of the woman, Stirrup, is called the urethra.'

The boys all looked at each other in disbelief. It didn't sound like that was the word. They'd not heard that word before. It didn't sound right.

I had a go.

'Miss, what is the part of the man's body called that he uses to go to the toilet?'

'The penis, Josie. It is called the penis.'

'Pee-nis.'

We laughed, the pee-nis and dangling balls, etched in our brains.

Only the sound of the second film rolling brought us back to the room. It showed a diagram of a penis being inserted into a vagina. My questions were for the most part answered. The baby growing in the stomach was all accounted for and milk in the breasts to feed it seemed like a sensible idea and reminded me of cows on a farm. What I didn't understand was why breasts had to swell up anyway, even if there wasn't any milk in them, and why the penis turned from soft to hard. What made it do that?

Stirrup asked Miss Barlow that last question but she wouldn't answer it. We all wanted to know what made it do that. Somebody muttered something about 'emotions' but never expanded upon it.

After the Sex Education class was over, there seemed no need, as far as I was concerned, to keep quiet about it. I particularly wanted to tease a boy called Malty who was in a lower class than me and who was sat ready and ripe for a spot of bother, on the gates of the school, when I left that afternoon. Me and this girl called Valerie dragged him off the gate and pinned him to the side of the school fence.

'Where's your penis, Malty?' I had him by the tie half choking him.

37

'I don't know. I haven't got one.'

We fell about laughing. I tightened my grip and snarled at him.

'You haven't got one. What are yer, a girl or somethin'? Where's your penis, I said.'

'I don't know. I don't know what yer on about, honest I don't.'

Valerie started on him.

'Do you want me to show yer where it is, Malty?'

'No, I don't.' It was slowly dawning on Malty where his penis might be.

'If yer don't show us it then we'll get it out ourselves.'

He was terrified.

I gave Malty a swift boot in the place where he expected his penis to be. Me and Valerie ran off home laughing.

My mum was a school cleaner. She arrived home some two hours after me. When I got home I had to haul up the key that was dangling on a piece of string on the back of the door. Once inside, I went straight to the kitchen in the hope. I never gave up hope. I always saw a wax-bagged loaf of bread and two pots of jam. I made my butties and a cup of tea and went to the front room to watch my daily dose of *Peyton Place*. By the time *Magpie* or *How* or *Crackerjack* was over, depending on what day it was, Mum would be home. She did things in the kitchen before settling down to watch the news. She usually came into the front room and said something about the school, what a mess it was, as though I was the only one that went there. This day though she came home and never said a word.

I heard my dad's van pull up about an hour later and the front door was open before he had a chance to put his key in the lock. I could hear muffled conversation dragging on in the hallway. Before I knew it I was lying in bed crying my eyes out with my backside on fire. The belt had slit into me like a knife. I didn't know what the hell was going on. I heard Martin come out of his bedroom and go downstairs. I heard him asking them what was wrong. Then I listened hard.

'She's been asking some lad where 'is Johnny is and then she's kicked him in his privates hard. The poor lad's not well. She's up in her room and she's stayin' up there till the mornin', the little bitch. I've a mind to tell the Canon about her. See what he thinks to it.'

'Tell the Canon about it. And the woman who carried me in her stomach and grew tits the size of spacehoppers to feed me. Tell her as well.' Under my breath.

When Bernadette came to bed I was ready for her.

'Have you ever had a willy inside your vagina?'

'Don't you think you've done enough damage today? Yer not s'posed to talk like that.'

'Well, they did at school today. They showed us pictures an' everythin'.'

'Never,' sarcastically.

'They did. We 'ad *Where Do Babies Come From?* and *Growing Up*. I saw pictures of a naked man and a woman. The woman looked like you 'cept she was white. She had loads of 'airs on her fanny – like you!'

'D'yer wanna 'nother look?'

'No thanks.'

Bernadette laughed.

'No, I've never had a willy up me vagina. Yer not s'posed

39

to do it till yer married. I've not even seen a willy yet, not a man's one anyway.'

'I have.'

'No you 'aven't. Whose 'ave you seen?'

'Martin's.'

'Yer shouldn't've been lookin', yer dirty cow. Don't let me mam know you've seen it – she'll give yer a right crackin'.'

'I know … Who's your mam? Who had you in her belly?'

'My mum was a nurse. From the Lake District. She gave me away.'

'Why did she give you away?'

'Because she wasn't married.'

'Why didn't she get married?'

'I don't know. Shut yer mouth and get to sleep.'

'D'yer think *my* mum and dad are dead?'

'Ask. Yer won't know unless yer ask.'

'OK. I will then. I'll ask.'

In the darkness I saw Martin's willy. It got bigger and bigger and was surrounded by bubbles. The magnitude of his sin revealed itself. I was party to that sin. I'd kept quiet about it for so long that I was as guilty as him for not saying anything. I was an accomplice.

That wasn't the end of it. At school the next day, Valerie and me were hauled into Mr Dowd's office and offered ten strokes of the ruler on the back of the legs or five of the cane on the hand. I went for the hand job. Valerie fainted. She was such a yellow babby.

Chapter 6

'Josie, can yer come downstairs, please?'

That wasn't right. On Saturday mornings. Waiting to get up. Usually it was 'Josie, yer can come down now', like the end of a game. Bernadette was already down there. She *had* to get up early. I didn't get that.

I pulled on the frock that was hanging over the end of the bed and brushed my hair out as best I could. Holding the walls either side of the stairs I crept down, listening out for a taste of what I was about to receive. Nothing. Silence. Then the pump.

Me mum was sat on the chair facing the window in the dining room. She sat there to get the full view of the top of the street. From our house upwards she could tell who was in, who was out, and where they were all off to. She didn't miss a trick. She was holding her little black pump, its bulb about the size of a small onion, collapsing with the clenching of her fist. It had a stem, about three inches long, of smoky-brown stained glass and a small mouthpiece bent for easy entry. It was like a baby musical instrument. As I walked into the room, she began to cough, then pump, then cough again. The orchestra was tuning up. Then just

41

a rhythmic pump with the metre of anxiety heaving in the background on her chest. PUMP pmmm, pmmm, heave, PUMP pmmm, pmmm, heave . . .

'Mornin',' I offered, testing the water, between the heave and the pump.

'Mornin',' PUMP pmmm, pmmm. Quiet. Then, 'Get that frock off, it's filthy. And get your school shoes down, they need cleanin'.' PUMP pmmm, pmmm.

I looked down at my frock. 'It's not that bad. I only wore it one day last week. Can I wear it? I'm not goin' anywhere.' To the kitchen.

She was too busy coughing. The school shoes were broke.

'Can I make a fresh pot?'

Bernadette came through the back door with a washing basket. She had to do her own washing. She was old enough, she was told.

'I'll make the tea,' she said. 'Go and sit yerself down.'

'You've got into the Convent School, although God knows how we're goin' to manage.' PUMP pmmm, pmmm.

'What Convent School?'

'The Loreto, in town. Yer passed your exam.'

'I never took an exam. Honest I didn't.'

'Yer did.'

'I didn't – honest.'

'Yer did, I'm tellin' yer.'

Bernadette came in with the tea. She looked like she felt sorry for me.

'I don't wanna be a nun.'

'You're not gonna be a nun. It's a school like any other school, only a damn sight more expensive. You've won a scholarship. It'd be criminal to turn it down. God knows

how yer've managed it. *I* certainly don't. We're not one for brains in this family so I guess your mother must've 'ad some somewhere. And God knows 'ow we'll manage.'
PUMP pmmm, pmmm.

'Manage?'

'The bloody uniform costs the earth. You'll 'ave to go to a special outfitter's in Liverpool an' all that. It says 'ere, you'll need hockey sticks and tennis rackets, multi-coloured knickers, indoor shoes and outdoor shoes. You'll need a proper briefcase, books and pens. It's gonna cost a bloody fortune. Wait till your father hears about this. He'll 'ave a bloody 'art attack.'

'Well, I don't 'ave to go, do I? I never did it on purpose. I know we can't afford indoor shoes *and* outdoor shoes, don't I?' I was thinking about the broken ones I'd hidden upstairs under the bed.

'We'll all 'ave to cut down, that's all.'

Bernadette piped up sullenly, 'Cut down any more an' we'll all be eatin' dock leaves.'

'Shut yer trap, yer little madam. You ought to be thankful yer eatin' at all, y'ungrateful little sod. Shame you've not got the brains to sort yerself out. If yer done with that washin' yer can get up to the shops.' She slammed a five-pound note on the table – like she'd been waiting for just the right moment. 'There's a list in the top drawer in the kitchen and you'll find there's no dock leaves on it either. Now, get out of me sight. Go on!'

Bernadette moved quickly. I heard Martin coming down the stairs. He went straight out of the front door with Bernadette. From the window, Mum and me watched the two of them walk up the street together.

'Where's our Gary?'

43

'Playin' football.'

'At 'ome or away?'

'He's away. He'll not be back till this afternoon. He needs new stuff 'n' all, and there's Bernadette's stuff to get. I'll not be able to manage. I'll 'ave to ask the Canon for more money. He gives us precious little, God knows, but if he wants you to 'ave this *good education* then I'm afraid 'e's the one who's gonna 'ave to fork out for it. I don't see why Gary should suffer on account o' you pair!'

'Mum, what does adoption mean?'

'It means that someone takes on a child as their own.'

'Am I adopted?'

'No. You're fostered.'

'Why aren't I adopted then? I've been 'ere for ages.'

'Oh, somethin' to do with your real mother signin' the papers.'

'Who's me real mother then? Where is she?'

'I don't know. They can't find her.'

'Why didn't she keep me then?'

'I don't know why she didn't keep yer. I expect she 'ad her reasons.'

'Was I found on a doorstep or somat like that – in a shoebox with a Paddington Bear message stuck on me?'

'You were taken to the Nazareth House and left there. That's all I know. Don't be sarcastic.'

'Then if she didn't want me, why didn't she sign the papers?'

'I don't know, Josie, I don't know.' PUMP pmmm, pmmm.

'Why did you want me?'

At that moment, the front door slammed. We were both silenced.

'Sounds like me dad, Mum.'

'No, it can't be, 'e's on ten till ten.'

I listened harder. The stair-creaks. The direction on the landing. Then I heard the familiar sound of his weight hitting the mattress springs. Only me dad's bed made that noise so I knew it was him.

'It is. It's him. It's his bed, I can tell.'

The coughing started again. She stood up quickly, throwing the pump on the dining-room table. She looked out of control. Unbalanced, she reached for the door handle, her face full of panic and worry. It upset me to see her like that. Like she was trying to hold on.

I listened hard from the bottom of the stairs for clues. But there was nothing, not for ages. And then, my mum's voice. All I heard was her weep of resignation, over and over again saying, 'But they'll say there's no smoke without fire, no smoke without fire, that's what they'll say.' And then more weeping.

They stayed in the bedroom until nightfall. Bernadette and me sneaked round the house doing all the chores. Then we watched sport on the telly, waiting for *Voyage to the Bottom of the Sea*.

They'd never done that before. Ever. Stayed in their room all day. Nobody disturbed them except Gary to tell his mum that he'd scored two goals and was now the captain of the football team. Gary wanted them downstairs acting normal again. He hovered around the foot of the stairs waiting for an apparition. When it came, I was sent to bed.

I lay for a long time trying to find situations where there was smoke without fire.

. . . Cigarettes . . . Benediction . . . aeroplanes . . . toast
. . . I fell asleep on it.

Boylie was impressed. 'Oh you'll go to university and
get a degree. That's what me mum said . . . what's a
degree, Josie?'

'I don't know but I'm glad there won't be any boys
there. I hate boys. And that includes you, Boylie.'

Chapter 7

Bernadette didn't last much longer. She started doing a milk round. Gettin' up at the crack o' sparrers deliverin' milk. She saved up her wages and then went and bought a dress that was 'up her arse' as me mum called it. Me mum pulled all the hem down so all the cotton bits hung down on her leg. I could still see the proper line where the real hem should have been. Bernadette was screaming when me mum did that. Me and me mum were in the dining room. Bernadette danced in really proud of her new frock and then did a little bow. Which made her dress seem even shorter from behind. Me mum went berserk. Dived on her. Started ripping away at the hem. Bernadette screamed and me, I threw far too much sugar over me Weetabix.

Then Bernadette did something really stupid. She stood there with her arms folded, dead cool and calm and collected. And really quietly she said, 'I hate you.'

They never spoke again after that day. Not properly.

When I was on me own with me mum, she said that midis were 'in'. She said that minis were 'out' and, if Bernadette had half a brain about her, she could have seen that for herself. But that wasn't true really. Midis were in on *Top of the Pops* but they were still wearing minis round our way. Me mum just said that so she could be even more right than she was. The dress *was* dead short.

After that Bernadette didn't care any more. Which left her wide open for Gary. Gary opened up a hairdresser's in the back shed, him playing the barber with dad's hedge shears. The sight of Bernadette's fat black plait sat tight between the blades of the shears made her faint. Which made him make a pretty bad job of it. So the next day she had her hair done properly in Mum's hairdresser's in the kitchen. She was crying her eyes out. And she kept talking gibberish all the time. Like some foreign language. And all that hair! I think that *that* was the end of what was later called Bernadette's 'stay with us'. Her hairs were everywhere after she'd gone. To keep reminding us. Even in the chip pan.

The battered suitcase that normally sat under the bunk beds was on top of the dressing table open and half full of clothes, most of which Bernadette would rather have set fire to. She pulled down the lid to examine her new crew cut in the mirror and she caught me staring at her from the bed. She turned around and put her head right up close.

'Yer know, it's not 'alf as bad at St Barny's as it is 'ere. All the kids really like each other and you can choose what to eat. Yer don't have to eat what you're given. And we get toothpaste. Not that brown bottle of peroxide stuff that makes yer want to be sick.'

'What about Christmas though? Yer don't get presents.'

'Rubbish! We get loads of presents. More presents than we know what to do with. We don't get big presents like bikes or anythin' like that but we get loads of stuff, new clothes, nice books, make-up for the girls. Loads of things. And pocket money. They give us pocket money.'

'But yer don't have a mum and dad though?'

'No, but yer don't need one really. We have housemothers and there's a few nuns that poke their noses in every now and again but everyone's always looked after. Shirley who sees to our house is great. She's got three of her own kids. They come in to see us.'

'But isn't it a bit like jail?'

'Well, isn't it here? You spend more time in this bedroom than you do downstairs. They don't leave you in your room for longer than two hours at Barny's – ever. Why don't yer tell Wilcox what they're really like? You *can* leave, yer know.'

I chewed it over. Barny's sounded all right really.

'What would I say? Oh I don't like it 'ere. I want to go to Barny's. Whoever 'eard of someone trying to break *into* an orphanage and anyway, they've been good to me. They were good to take me. I can't just leave coz of Christmas pressies and pocket money.'

'Look, Josie. There's more to it than that. I've heard yer talking in yer sleep, yer know.'

'Oh yeah! What sayin'?'

I didn't believe her. But then I didn't really know what I got up to when I was asleep. It was weird thinking that I was still alive when I was asleep. I'd heard about people that walked around in their sleep. Went to town an' that. So she could have been telling the truth.

'You were talking about willies. And me dad. And Martin.'

'Yer lyin' cow.'

'Yer were, Josie, I 'eard yer. More than once, an' all.'

'I'm gonna tell me mum on you.'

'When I told Mrs Wilcox that I wanted to leave, she asked me things. About me dad. I said *I* didn't have a problem with me dad. More with me mum and Gary. And me hair.'

Bernadette looked me straight in the eye when she said it, like she was definitely lying. I always did that when I was lying. To make it look like I was telling the truth. She got it off me. Me mum said the truth comes straight out. She said lyin' takes a bit longer coz it has to go round the houses.

'Has anyone asked you anythin'?' Looking me in the eye again.

'Asked me what? I don't know what you're on about.'

'It doesn't matter.' She went back to the dressing table, deflated.

I put my head under my pillow but I was still watching her, peeping. Why did she go on about her hair all the time? It was nicer than mine. No reason to pack yerself off to an orphanage. OK, Mum did it a bit wonky, and it wasn't anywhere near as good as before Gary chopped all the best bits off, but what about mine? Mum cut my hair the way the gardeners do the hedges at Hatton Park. Standing back every five minutes to see the shape. That's where Gary got the idea, I think. Of using Dad's shears. The gardeners did chickens and stars and Christmas bells in Hatton Park. Mum wasn't anywhere near that good.

I got the feeling they were gonna send me to Barny's whether I liked it or not. Bernadette ('Burn-her-to-death', our Gary called her) was trying to get me to say something.

I knew that if I did say anythin' I'd definitely go to Barny's. I reckoned she was lying about the presents and the pocket money and the happy housemothers. It was no good being an orphan, locked away in a big building. Like lepers. I didn't wanna be one. And if it *was* so good at Barny's, why did Martin always say that that was where they'd send me if I told? It couldn't have been that good. He should know coz he was a grown-up.

She blew up again. Refuelled. As if she had a great idea, she turned round smiling. The way grown-ups smile at little kids.

'Listen, Josie . . . just remember this. You can leave here whenever you like. Barny's 'll 'ave yer. Write to me. Tell me everything. Anything. Anything that's happened. If you're upset or lonely or anything. Will yer do that? Will yer promise to write to me?'

'Yeah, course I will.'

Mum was right. She was a troublemaker.

The smoke was worrying the eyes off me mum. They were constantly red and watery. I saw a letter about free dinners on the sideboard. I think she was worried about 'managing'. That's all I ever heard when I was listening when I shouldn't have been. 'How are we going to manage?' Micky Green's mum and dad couldn't manage because he had to have free dinners. But Micky Green had fifteen brothers and sisters. There were sixteen till Smudger died. There was only me and Gary after Bernadette went. If I had to have free dinners then we *definitely* couldn't manage. So there was no smoke without fire.

There weren't many rows any more because everybody stopped talking to each other. Just fights between Gary and me. Proper fights. Nosebleed fights. Arm-breaking fights. Drop-dead fights.

Chapter 8

Martin's baritone piss tap was pouring away in the loo. I could tell it was his, slightly softer than Dad's, but stronger than Gary's and not as melodic as Mum's. Everyone has a piss identity. I took a pillow and smothered my face in it. The smell of Bernadette was still there, like the seaside after a holiday. I wanted Bernadette back. It was partly my fault she left. I didn't stick up for her very well.

I felt the pillow move away from me. I sat up with the shock. I thought it was her, Bernadette. It was Martin.

'Come with me.'

'Where to?'

'Into me room.'

'Me mum and dad are downstairs. They'll hear me.'

'That's all right. They're watching *Callan*. They'll never hear us.'

'But I don't want to. I want to go to sleep.'

'Come on,' he said, searching beneath the blankets for my hand. He found it and half pulled me out of the bed. I pulled back. If I made my own way I'd be quieter.

It was like he was the child and I was the grown-up.

The room that was Gran's was utterly transformed. The

walls were painted a sky blue all over and over the sky blue were psychedelic curls of spiralling circles in pink, orange, green and lemon. Some of the curls were joined up with others and then there were others that had a life of their own. On one wall there was the trunk of a tree and around it a snake was curling its way up to the ceiling. There was fire falling from the forked tongue of the snake and the redness in the fire ruined the whole picture. His bed had no legs – just a mattress on the floor. There were black cloths hanging over the pelmets for curtains.

He pulled both of the black curtains down to cover the windows and turned on a red lamp that lit up the snake a treat. Then the fiery tongue looked really convincing.

'Do you wanna listen to some music?'

'OK.'

'Which one would you like?'

'Mmm, "Tap Turns on the Water".'

'No, I don't wanna play that one. It's too loud. Think of another.'

'Errr, "Where Do you Go To, My Lovely?"'

'OK.'

He fixed the record player so it was just loud enough for him to hear a disturbance downstairs, the ballbearing leaving the hole in the front-room door. He turned towards me. He took down my pyjama bottoms. He sat on the bed and pulled me towards him and felt me. I didn't budge.

I watched the spiralling curls on the walls and followed each one in turn playing a maze game. Every time I came to a dead end I began another curl and followed it around the room. He was pulling me down. He wanted me to kneel down. I knelt down. He steered my hand towards him. I wouldn't look down. I continued mazing the walls. I felt the rod.

A stale smell singed my nostrils. He guided my hand up and down the rod. My hand was limp though. He squeezed my hand around the rod and made me grip it and then pulled it up and down.

The skin on the rod moved with my hand. I pulled my hand away. He pulled it back again and I felt the tip of the rod. It was wet. The smell made me retch.

He knelt up and tried to put it inside me. Like they did in the picture at school. He was pushing it inside me and I cried out and he slapped his hand right across my mouth and snot poured out of my nostrils. And tears down my face. Nearly sick. And whining like an animal. And angry that I didn't know what was going on.

So where do you go to . . .

'Josie, is that you?' My mum was shouting from the bottom of the stairs. The adverts must've come on.

'It's all right, Mum,' Martin shouted down. 'I'm just waiting for her to come out of the bathroom.'

He stood in the doorway holding up a lollipop.

Chapter 9

Her hair was so thin it looked as though the top layer had
fallen off leaving just an underblanket. On the whole she
was quite a woman, lanky Twiggy-style and modern. She
had determined spots that she tried to hide with crusts of
pink stuff that fell off in clumps on to her tight jumpers.
She smelt like the chemist's. She had a loud cackling laugh
and talked about nothing in particular all the time. And she
was a Proddy dog. I was glad Martin was getting married.
Because the next time he went too far.

It was a Saturday and I was trying to do my stair job again
with the battered brush. I don't know why she didn't just get
a new brush. They couldn't have been that expensive. She
could have nicked one from the school. They had loads.
Laughing and tickling me, Martin chased me up the stairs.
He caught me on the landing, bent down and looked into
my eyes. I thought he was asking for forgiveness. From
the lollipop time. He drowned me. Weighed his body over
me – wrapped himself all around me and lifted me with
mechanical ease. Expecting comfort, I felt easy. I put my
arms around his spotty neck and nuzzled into his crick
– betrayed. He thrashed about urgently. His arms were

rigid. I clung to him like a monkey, not realising, and then he pushed his rod between my legs. I felt the pressure of it driving through the drumskin. The puncture pain delved as a malevolence. He knew he'd gone too far.

Six weeks later he was married and gone. He only came back for ham butties on a Sunday after that. Not every Sunday. Like a visitor. And for the christenings. He had two baby girls, one of them with a cleft palate rhyming with mallet, sounding like something out of the shed.

I wanted to tell. But I couldn't. I was just twelve. How could I tell after all that time? For years it went on. And anyway, Dad was having troubles of his own. I wanted to tell him something that'd cheer him up. Get closer to him. But it wasn't right. Wasn't done, that getting closer stuff.

He fought for his life and his country, Dad told me. In Burma, wherever that is. That was why he was a nobody. Because he didn't go to school properly, he thought he was a nobody. But he wasn't a nobody really. He taught himself most things. Like maths and stuff. Well, adding and subtracting. He couldn't do algebra or anything like that. But coz of his head for maths he was the tombola man three nights a week. On another night, he was the chairman of the Tenants' Association. He fought for a better council estate, better facilities. And better policing. He visited the sick and made reports for local council meetings. And when he wasn't doing any of that he was working and sleeping.

I was in the bathroom when I heard them – rowing in whispers.

'Look, Margaret, I've been workin' for the Lecky for twenty-two years and it doesn't seem to count. My days are numbered. They'll not 'ave me back now, so don't build up yer 'opes.'

He was the string vest and rolled-up sleeves type, pulled-down braces and a knotted hanky protecting his bald head sat on the beach in the sun. 'Cept he never sat on a beach and certainly wouldn't have sat in the sun because it made him come out in a rash. He had 'I love you' tattoos up his arms. That blue ink staining his arm was the only hard physical display I ever . . . that was as close to the surface as it was going to get anyway.

'It's wicked. Innocent till proven guilty, that's what justice is. British justice, anyroads. What do they think they're playin' at? How are we s'posed to manage?'

'They'll pay me till I'm finished.'

'But that's not the point. What'll 'appen then? After you're finished?'

'I don't know. I don't bloody know. Leave off, will yer.'

'If I find out. If I find out there's the slightest truth to this then it'll be the end of us. I can't promise I'll stay!'

'Listen to yerself!' he shouted – whispering. 'You're worse than them. Don't believe me, do yer? Think I did it, don't yer? Yer don't even trust your old man. You're upsettin' me now, Marg. I think yer better shut up.'

'It's not I don't believe yer. It's just, well, what'll everyone think? She shouldn't have been there in the first place, should she? Why d'yer pick her up? Why, for God's sake? Even if you're not guilty. It doesn't matter round 'ere. As I said before there's no smoke . . .'

I was painting my toenails and making a bad job of it.

When I was as finished as I could be I opened all the windows and pulled the chain. As I left the bathroom, my mum put her head round the door.

'What are yer doin' sneakin' round at this hour of the mornin', and what's that smell?'

'It's nothin'.'

'Yes it is. It's nail varnish. Let me see yer 'ands.'

I showed my snowy fingertips. Like a magician, I secreted the bottle of varnish beneath my hand but she spotted the trick and turned my hand over.

'Now then. Where d'yer get this, might I ask?'

'It's not mine. It's Lucy's.'

'So what are *you* doin' with it?'

'She lent it to me. To put on me feet.'

I pushed my good foot forward.

'Yer look like a tart. Now get it off.'

'I can't. I 'aven't got any remover.'

'Well, I have. Just you wait there.'

'But why?'

'Because it's tarty and you're not old enough for this stuff yet, not by a long chalk, so don't argue!'

She came back with a bottle of surgical spirit.

'Mum, why isn't Dad going to work?'

'Who said he wasn't?'

'Well, there isn't any shirt on the back of the bathroom door and he never went to work yesterday either.'

'It's 'is teeth,' she said in staccato.

'What's 'is teeth?'

'He's got toothache and he's 'avin' all 'is teeth out today.'

''Ere, Dad!' I was shouting through the crack in the door. 'Me mum said yer 'avin' all yer teeth out. Do they 'urt?'

'Don't ask such bloody stupid questions. Of course they 'urt. I wouldn't be 'avin them out else, would I?'

'No, s'pose not.' Then I piped up again.

"'Ow yer gonna tell whose is whose teeth? You'll 'ave to put labels on the glasses in the bathroom so yer don't get 'em mixed up. Eh! I wonder if me mum's teeth 'd fit yer? 'Ave yer tried 'em? They might, yer know.'

'Josie, why don't you mind your business and shut it, will yer!'

'Mum?'

'You heard.'

When I came home from school he was sat in the dining room. Without teeth his face looked like a deflated tyre. Like someone had took the wind out of him. Sad. Not talking. I imagined each root torn from the soft gum, the branches twisting and breaking the skin. I thought of the cold air wafting on his sore hollows and the warm flow of blood trickling and collecting in his throat, gagging him. And I saw his mouth full of fresh air and blood. Some of the blood dribbled to form a mosaic of brown crust on his bottom lip.

He refused to leave the house until his new teeth were made up and then until he'd got used to them. Across the dining table there were flying teeth for almost three weeks. That's why he was home all the time.

With some practice he was talking like his old self again nearly. He still didn't go to work or to the tombola and tenants' meetings. He just stayed in. He didn't even do the garden. He slept in Martin's room. There were no Sunday dinners and no explanations. At church he stood at the back with the men that give out the collection plates. And he never went to communion. He did Confession though the day before. He was in there for ages. Sometimes I wished that I was Father Brady because at least then I'd have known what was going on. His new teeth made him look like someone was working him from behind.

I was glad they weren't doin' the tombola because when they did I was left in the house with Gary on my own. All his mates came round and I had to play slave. I was scared all day right up until Mum and Dad picked up the shopping bags full of bingo tickets. And then she said, 'Bed at eight for her,' meaning me. As soon as they were down the path and in the van, Gary started on me. The boys arrived. And it was roller-coaster from then on. Anything could happen. Gary told the boys that I wasn't his real sister. Said I was from a kids' home. So that gave them the right, if you like.

Sometimes I thought about going over to Martin's place and telling him. He lived on the new estate on the other side of the woods. I missed him. I did go round and see him once but he was really off with me. So I didn't think there was any point going round there snitching.

The boys. I wasn't scared of them when they were on their own, as individuals. They were OK then. It was when they did things together – bovver boys, they called themselves. The way they gee-ed each other up was frightening. I thought one of them was dead once. He just lay there with loads of blood pouring out of his head. Turned out that he fainted on account of his heavy nose bleed after a head-butt. I wanted everything back to normal but I didn't want the tombola nights back. Ever.

For three mornings in a row Dad went out in a suit. It was Uncle Eddie's old suit. I could tell it wasn't his. It didn't fit him, for starters. And it smelled funny.

'Where's me dad goin', Mum – in a suit?'

'Mind this,' pointing to her nose.

'I was just wond'rin'.'

61

'Well, we all know what wond'rin' did, don't we?'

'No.'

'Don't cheek me, young lady. Now mind your business like I said and let your father mind his.'

On the third day he came home with flowers. He never *bought* flowers. He grew them. Was he mad? Suits and flowers.

And that day Father Brady came round to see us. Mum got him to bless the house again. To make it like new, she said. He went in every room. They stayed in the dining room all night, Mum and Dad. On their own. I heard me mum say, after Father Brady left, that she'd help Dad move his things back into their bedroom but he said he didn't want to bother. I heard him say there was no point since they slept in their own beds anyway. I didn't get that. When I went in to get a drink of water I saw Mum looking down at her hands. She was rolling her hands round and round, really nervously. Then she got her pump out and started playing pummmp-pummmp sounds in the quietness.

When I got back in the front room I heard me dad say that he missed his mum. Over and over again he said it, yarling.

'But, Margaret, I didn't know I'd miss her like this. God, I miss her. God, I loved me mum.'

And it was only then that I realised that Gran *was* his mum. I never, before then, thought about me dad's mum, making his tea and hugging him as a baby. Gran wasn't like that. She was hard-faced and didn't knit fluffy jumpers. Cold. But he missed her. Me dad missed her.

Coz the house had just been blessed we couldn't put the telly on so we heard everything. Like telly fasting, I thought.

After an hour or so, me mum came in and saw us sat there, bewildered. She'd forgotten that we weren't watching telly. Forgotten the little rule that she'd made up and slipped in to make the house feel even holier, after Father Brady left, trying to hang on to the echoes of his blessing. When she realised we must have heard everything, she practically ordered us to put the telly back on. I think I saw a tear fall from our Gary's eye.

'What's up?' I said. To let him know that I saw. And to find out what was up.

'Shut it,' he said.

When I went in for another drink of water, I caught them holding hands. I'd never seen that before. They stayed there all night talking. They didn't even come in to watch *Coronation Street*. They weren't even listening to the radio. And she did the ironing. Later on, after I was sent to bed, I listened on the stairs to what was going on.

'Ernie turned up.'

'He never.'

'Aye.'

'Wanted to hear it from the horse's mouth, I expect.'

'Well, he might o' lent me his suit but he still thought I was guilty.'

'What did he say after?'

'Said he'd known I was innocent all along. 'S easy to say that after, int it, eh? Spect most of 'em are sayin' that now. Still he 'ad to ask me why I picked her up. Still a trace o' doubt there, I could tell.'

'What d'yer say to him?'

'Same as I said to you. She looked like she was in trouble. *She* came on to me. The court agreed, for Christ's sake. Ten bloody minutes. After all that worryin' it took 'em

63

ten bleedin' minutes. If I ever clap eyes on that woman again I'll do for her. I'll be back in court . . .'

'What did Father Brady say when yer was seein' him off at the gate?'

'Said if I wanted to go back and do the tombola I could.'

'And?'

'Well, after the way they shut us out like that . . . Jesus Christ! I was guilty as sin as far as they were concerned.'

She did the ironing till gone ten o'clock. All his work shirts. On my third glass of water she didn't even tell me off. She was doing the orange curtains then.

Later on I heard Dad moving his stuff back into the bedroom. I heard all the coat hangers clanging. The clanging sounded peaceful.

Next day he was gone before I was out of bed. He was back on shifts.

Chapter 10

School. I destroyed lessons. Only the Latin mistress could hold me, could lick a whip of the tongue faster than I. I was brilliant at Latin . . . *bellum* . . . *bellum* . . . *bellum* . . . bla . . . bla . . . bla. None of the other teachers could go the full forty minutes. They were scared of me. They attacked. They sent letters to my parents. They fired them off in rapid succession, each one weakening the hold that Mum and Dad had over me. Oh sure, they held me. They imprisoned me. But they didn't have me.

It wasn't like before the war when girls were supposed to help their mothers peel spuds, wearing great big navy-blue knickers. How I wished there was a war on. But this was the seventies. Up until I was thirteen things weren't so bad. Then they brought out the Osmonds and the Jacksons and youth clubs with discos. Not discothèques. Discos. They brought out really little knickers and platform shoes. They brought out loads of magazines with huge posters inside. They brought out fancy record players, concerts, hot pants and lip gloss. All of it was brought out and paraded in front of me and I couldn't have any of it. Me being a Catholic protected from the opposite sex.

So I wrote diaries of events that never happened, of intimate encounters with boys that never existed, of love. Such recreation was hard work. There was no time or need to learn Latin. No point finding out why the French wanted rid of the bourgeoisie. I had no idea why MPs went to the Chiltern Hundreds or what the triangle of trade was all about. I needed to fit in. My body had other ideas. No matter how good my stories were, my body had the last say.

I prayed to God for three things. Straight hair, straight-down hips and fried-eggs tits. I was rewarded with vastness on every landscape and a fuzzy head. My friends matched my vision of perfection precisely. Some had the nerve to want bigger tits. This, when I was having difficulty carrying mine around. They say kids are insensitive but bloody hell.

After my body lost its childhood everything seemed to slow down. Between lessons I walked in slow motion, the younger kids hurtling past in another world. Anything that involved 'action' seemed frightening. I wanted to hibernate.

Then everyone wanted to know what I was gonna be. Curiously, I think they were worried. They couldn't see me anywhere. In the navy. In an office block. In a factory. And I couldn't either. I started to worry myself. I wanted to know. What was I gonna be?

'And what yer gonna be when yer grow up, young lady?'

Because I was fifteen they really meant it. Not like when I was little, holding on to shopping trolleys.

'And what yer gonna be when yer grow up, young lady?'

The women in their *cappuccino* macs with chocolate buttons on, the size of an old penny. I still remember their heads in shiny flowered scarves tied tight under their chins so their faces to me were those of giant puppets with no ears. Some had lumps on their chins like unripe raspberries, hard and stuck on. They were strangers in the supermarket. Big strangers who wanted to know who I was. What was I like. Like I was a Ronnie Redman. The thalidomide kid from near the park. 'Aaaaaaahh.' 'Loooooook!' As if there was something wrong with me. Just because I was brown.

'What yer gonna be?'

'I want to be an air 'ostess.' I always said that. All the other little girls said that.

Then the women and their puppet faces broke into smiles and 'Aah's and 'Ooh's and licking lips to eat me. Swallowing my English mother tongue.

'Oh! You want to travel a lot then? Fly away to exotic places?'

Like mops and brushes put away for the day they finished the conversation right there. Stood upright. Job done.

The 'air hostesses didn't travel to exotic places round our way. When I went to the chipper on a Friday night I saw them stood at the bus stop outside the 'airdresser's. They had big handbags with comb-handle daggers sticking out of the side – their hair piled up high like Rolos.

No one round our way became doctors or detectives, or air hostesses, for that matter. I saw girl-women in earrings and make-up. I walked past them standing on corners in giggling groups, listening to tinny transistors. Bare-armed and cold. I saw tired womeny-women with prams and pushchairs and kids on leads half falling off the backs of buses. Mad. And then the puppets in their scarves. Zipped bags of shopping. Rolling trolleys of food. Marching into wind. Lonely and dull. No make-up. No earrings. No choice.

By fifteen my brain and my body knew well enough I didn't want to be anything at all. There weren't any places or spaces where my body felt comfortable. Except in bed. There I could sink. Hidden. No demands. No arguments. Out of bed, I felt like a tree with no branches. Even in the bathroom, supposedly a haven, a stronghold, a private inspection room, a place to go to pamper pimples. I didn't fit or like it in there. I didn't have pimples. The bath never filled with hot water. Never sprung as a Zealand Geyser. Natural – surging – steamy geyser for a Maori me as I learned in geography and so much wanted to be. That's what I wanted to be, a bloody Maori. But the hot tap strained. It resented giving. Dribbling just enough to make a sound like a pee. After half an hour a scalding puddle at the bottom of the bath to singe the buttocks. A channel in a white valley vat. Cold breasts without lapping warm water to jostle about in. The body didn't fit. It should have been thinner, flatter, whiter, smoother – less stark, less bark.

Then, after watching Margaret Lockwood in a court-room drama on TV, I fantasised a barrister. Wig and all. (A crocheted doily from the princess's dressing table.) In defence of the accused. Standing on my bed to make myself look tall for the jury, hand on hip, I speak:

The judge has asked that you disregard the evidence you have just heard from the prosecution, as such evidence, if indeed it so be called, does not have any relevance to this case. I would ask one more thing. Do not think of a green horse. Put the green horse out of your mind. Indeed, I am sure you would agree – the green horse is not relevant to this case. Thank you.

I sit down and tuck my knees up under my chin and wait to hear the verdict. And of course I win. After Margaret Lockwood did it, I saw green horses charging round the house, catching buses and waiting for me outside school.

I was fat and fifteen and stood at the back of the chip queue. The nuns, never short on imagination, were selling chips from the library window. Fund-raising. Private funds were drying up. Comprehensives all the rage.

The playground stank of chips. Severe warnings about litter detentions were pasted up all over the trees like 'Wanted' posters. There was newspaper everywhere, flying about like kites laughing. The sky was nearly black. It was going to rain hard. The wind said so. Siobhan came over to join me. She was Irish. She got shot with a rubber bullet in Derry. She brought it to school to show us – so we believed her.

''Ave yer read this?'

She was holding up a copy of the *Ramsworth Reporter*. A really old copy that had had chips in it. Marella and co. were stood behind her – just in my line of view. She started to read, holding on to the paper in the wind as a sailor holds a boat in a storm:

Mr M. Milner of 17 Duchy Street, Ridgehill was today found Not Guilty of indecently assaulting a fifteen-year-old girl. Mr Michael Milner admitted giving the girl (who can't be named) a lift in a van belonging to the Electricity Board. After . . .

I only heard the first bit. That bit kept repeating itself in my brain. Indecent assault. Decent meant clothed. Indecent meant unclothed.

Siobhan was still blabbing.

'And look when it was.'

She held the paper over for me to see.

The wind blew the words of the story up to me. I couldn't see the date, only a picture of a woman in a bathing costume. And I saw the word 'indecent' and then the wind blew the paper out of her hand. She held on with the other hand and got the paper back again.

'Look when it was,' she repeated, holding up the corner with the date on, against the wind.

Her greasy fingers had all but dissolved the date except for the month and the year. It was over three years old, the newspaper! All that time it had been sat at the bottom of the art-room painting cupboards. And I helped carry those newspapers over to the library. They made me. The nuns. They said I never helped with anything. I was big and strong.

I remembered my mum ironing the orange curtains. I remembered the tombola stopping . . .

'Yer never said not'in' about that now, did yer?' Siobhan was grinning, I could swear it.

I looked again. The story was next to another story about Miss Ramsworth. There in her bathing costume. Miss Ramsworth used to go to our school. She was a prefect. A cruel one. Made us whiten her pumps in our dinner hour. Someone had painted a moustache on her and coloured in her pubes. They must have seen the 'INDECENT' headline alongside it. The 'NOT GUILTY OF INDECENT ASSAULT' headline. Miss Ramsworth had really big tits. Siobhan let go of the newspaper. There was just me holding it. She left me standing there on my own. The queue was nearly up to the library window and two young first-years were behind me, trying to see what I was reading.

'Are you in the queue?' one of them said, still trying to read.

I turned to see where Siobhan was. She was over by Marella's lot. Smiling at me. Smiling at me standing on my own, standing there holding the greasy newspaper . . . like it was me that shot her with that rubber bullet and she'd just got me back. Marella, Linda, everyone. They were laughing with their hands over their mouths and turning in on themselves. Away from me. I ran the playground and out so fast I was scared I was gonna fall over and make it all worse. I let the newspaper join the rest of the kites. I don't know whether they ran after it or not. Or after me even. I didn't look back.

I ran into the museum. My dad was in there. In a photo. In the war. With a gun. Pretending. Indecent assault . . . a not-guilty green horse kicking the shit out of me. Stamping its feet. Blocking my exits and entrances. I couldn't go out. I couldn't stay in. And I still had my indoor shoes on. No smoke without fire. The house a fucking inferno.

Out the back way. And I ran. Not out of fear. Not out of anything. For to be me, I suppose. For to make my heart beat so loud I could hear me, the real me – not all the noise around. The wind was behind me. I ran straight into a pillow. Head on. A pillow carried by a black man. He asked me the way to Ruddle's.

The first one I ever spoke to. He was proper black. A lot of people called me black but I'm brown really. Sometimes

I was called coloured like God had to use up those brown crayons on someone. The only time I used dark-brown crayons was for colouring in tree trunks. Sometimes I was called half-caste. Half-done.

This man was so dark brown he was black. Shiny black. I imagined the early adventurers bumping into such black people in the jungles. Coming back to England waving their pink hands up in the air, their noses red with burst blood vessels against faces white as sheets, scurvied and pock-marked. I saw their toothless jowls stretching from ear to ear as they charged into bars and taverns. Giving out descriptions of black fiends in dark jungles with wild white eyes and legs as long as oars. Monsters. I could understand them thinking that. Looking at this man. This man was a monster.

I looked at his face like a child looking up a mountain. He had a large mouth full to the brim with teeth. Frightening white teeth. His nose splattered right across his face. His lips, when he wasn't smiling, hung out over his chin. His eyes did the smiling. Even with his mouth shut and the lips turned down, his eyes still smiled. The whites of his eyes poked around in the black surrounding terrain and smiled. I talked to his eyes. They were full of welcome. Shiny eyes.

We went to a café.

'And so, Sister Josephine – you don't mind my calling you Sister, do you? Ah. Good. So tell me . . . what part of the world does your family come from?'

'Er, Ramsworth.'

'Yes, you live here but where do you come from? Which country?'

Either Africa, South America or the West Indies, I figured. Or even an island in the Pacific. I was definitely not a Maori. I'd gone off Maoris by then. I usually told people that I was from the Caribbean. That gave them a bit of a holiday. They went off for a couple of seconds under palm trees sun-bathing. I liked watching their faces when they did that. To Matthew, I couldn't decide if it was Jamaica or Papua New Guinea. I spotted Papua New Guinea just that week on a map of the world in Geography.

'I don't know.'

'You do not know where your family comes from. Dat is a strange idea.'

'I don't know anythin'.'

I told him a short and censored life story, only stopping to pick off the skin from the mug of milky coffee that was still two-thirds full. When I was finished, the natural laws of conversation took over and I had to listen to him. What a saga! Princes and kings, aeroplanes and cities far away, large, large families that lived in the heat by the sea where cars weren't needed and cigarettes weren't smoked. I sucked violently on the one he gave me. Grown-up.

'Would you like to come back to my place and see pictures of my family?'

'Oh yes please.' I was drunk on the coffee. Spaced out on the nicotine.

His fingers were long skeletal tools for picking things up. Perfect. With perfect white-moon nails tipping shiny black creaseless skin. He hadn't done a stroke in his life, I could tell. He squeezed my hand in his. It wasn't a good fit. No coupling there. My instinct for danger was asleep, zapped by the fistful of pound notes he kept taking out of his pocket.

73

'So, den, Sister Josephine. What is the rest of your programme for today?'

'Are there any starvin' people where you come from?'

'Yes . . . but there are hungry people everywhere. And . . . well, it's all relative, you know?'

'What's relative?'

'Well. Let me see . . . in England there are poor people that are suffering, no? Well, wherever they are, the poor will suffer.'

'I don't think there's anything relative about starving to death.'

'Indeed.'

He looked down at his hands.

'You're rollin' in it, aren't yer? I can tell by yer 'ands.' I pointed to his hands because he didn't seem to understand. 'Rich,' I said, pointing.

'I'm from a wealthy family. But I am studying medicine so I can help the poor of my country. So I can do something.'

'What country did yer say?'

'Nigeria.'

'Whereabouts in Africa's that? Is it near the Equator?'

'Closer to it than England.'

I thought he was a bit overdressed. He had a suit on and a great big camel coat over the top of it. It was summer.

Out in the street life was wild. Before I went into the café, people were out of my reach. Almost instantly the city had become a new world. Exciting. Each person a potential playmate. I was big enough to play with people. A world of endless possibilities drove past me in cars and walked in and out of public houses. What a lady I was! When I

74

climbed into the limo I waved like the Queen. He didn't get that. He was looking to see who I was waving at. It was a good fifteen minutes before the taxi stopped. Blasé and flamboyant, I jumped out of the cab like it was my hundredth that day.

The road was a cul-de-sac of large houses. Each had at least three floors and some more than that. After paying the cab driver, Matthew struggled towards a house, dropping his blankets in the street to find his keys. The house he chose was enormous, with double-breasted bay windows, white from tip to toe with a front garden you couldn't swing a gnome in.

I imagined its insides. Great halls of elegance with balustrades fit for the King. He told me he was a prince. The monster had taken a hike.

I imagined heavy velvet curtains and silver salvers littered across walnut sideboards. Deep rich swallowing red carpets warming the stairs and the lounge. Exotic cushions flung and scattered idly about the place, silks across the couches, good enough to hang in glasses.

The front door wouldn't open fast enough. The lock was stuck at first and then, when it did open, the door got stuck on bits of ragged carpet that were reproducing themselves in the porchway. I found myself in a vast hallway not dissimilar to the one I imagined but with everything missing. The balustrades must have looked all right some time back. The house felt empty. A big house for one man. I waited to be shown into a lounge. He fiddled around for more keys and went upstairs.

I couldn't understand why he needed to lock doors *inside* the house. To guard against untrustworthy servants? I used to watch *Upstairs, Downstairs* then. He opened a door wide

– wider than he needed to – so I figured that everything I'd imagined would be in there, inside that door. He signalled for me to go on in. Like I was a princess.

The room was occupied by a double bed. The rest of Matthew's life was around it. A shower with a dirty white curtain, mouldy black at the bottom. There was a sink on a wall which was full to the brim with soap boxes, flannels, shaving stuff, aftershave, nail scissors, wallets and other things. There was even a cooker in there. A Wendy-house cooker. Just two rings for cooking on and a little cupboard underneath for the oven. All this was on one side of the bed. The other side had a wardrobe and chest of drawers. On top of the chest of drawers were loads of photographs of black people, black women with things on their heads, black men in suits and ties, small children wearing all the colours of the world. The door closed behind me. I jumped.

Matthew took his shoes off. No socks. Socks would have kept him warmer. Did he know that English people wore socks, I wondered? He pulled out an enormous pair of black feet. His big toe looked like a rhinoceros's thumb. He used this to press the 'play' button on a small cassette recorder on the floor behind the door. Loud foreign music noised up from the ground. That big toe frightened me. The niftiness of its action. I began to imagine the niftiness of the whole man, not just his toe.

'Come, sit with me here on the bed and I will show you pictures from Africa. Nigeria . . .' He said the jeer in 'geria' dead geerily.

He had tons of photograph albums. I didn't want to sit on the bed but there wasn't anywhere else. He kept moving closer and closer. Photograph album covering his

76

legs. I wanted to be interested in the pictures but I could only see his hands and his toes.

'Here is brother Thomas graduating from some American university and . . .'

'Do you like England?' I asked, trying to make an interview out of it.

He looked at me like I was supper. I felt like supper.

'I wanna go to the toilet.'

'Ah, of course. Pardon me for not off'ring you earlier. I will show you the way.'

On the way out he did his big-toe trick again to turn the tape off.

I stood in the toilet thinking and deciding. I couldn't just run off without my blazer. I could. I didn't want to. But I did. When I got to the front door I couldn't open it. It was either stuck or locked or both. He was on me. He put his long arms on each side of my shoulder, his hands pressed against the wall. I looked up at his face and coming towards me was the pinkest tongue . . . I moved my head out of its way. I shook my head so he couldn't make contact again. He still had his hands pressed against the wall. Playing with his kill.

'Please don't kiss me.' I was covering my mouth with my arm. Looking up. Yarling.

'Apologies.' He took his hands from the wall and put them in his pockets instead. And then stood back. 'I didn't want to frighten you. You look very frightened.' Sincerely surprised, he was. I couldn't help but like him then. 'I thought you were something quite different,' he said, swaying and smiling with his hands in his pockets.

'What d'yer mean?' I asked, wiping my eyes.

'Never mind. Shall we try again. I promise no kissing. Cross my heart. Believe me?'

I had to believe him. I wanted to believe him. He didn't have much space but I needed it badly. We went back up the stairs. From under the bed he pulled out a little stool and pointed for me to sit on it. Then he made a cup of tea. It took ages.

'And so tell me about your unhappiness.'

'I can't.'

'Fine. Fine. Then do something for me.'

'What?'

'Try and spend this time with me being happy.'

'I'll try.'

'Good.'

He put Carnation milk in the tea and it tasted horrible.

'Why don't yer use proper milk?'

'This is nice milk, no?' He seemed to think it was a luxury.

'It's all right on peaches.'

'You want peaches?'

'No.'

I laughed then. I realised that everything I said was literal to him. He didn't know about the bits underneath my words, my thoughts. Well, I thought he didn't.

For three days we played. At home they'd be wondering, I knew. Maybe even worrying. Of course they'd be worrying. They'd be worrying about what to tell the Canon. I was glad to give them something to worry about.

He bought me clothes. And shoes. He watched the transformation with gentleness and the giddiness of a child. The new feelings he gave me changed the shape of my face, my mouth. Made me look at his face, his mouth. It was like being given the globe to look into. He let me explore the whole of his head. His nutty-shaped eyes, the smoothness all around his temples. The hint of pink blood colouring his blackness. Leaking into the whites of his eyes. It was the smoothness that got to me. His complexion was perfect, his chin sculptured out of pure matter. His hair was like a Brillo pad. Hard and springy but shaped to his head like it was part of his skin. A black skull cap. The first young man I'd come eye to eye with.

I reminded him of someone. He looked at my profile. He steadied my hands. I was nervous on the first night, when it was dark, when we'd finished the photo albums. He gave me his bed, his new pillow and new sheets. He got down on the floor and wrapped himself up in a pink candlewick bedspread, fully clothed.

'This doesn't seem fair,' he said.

I giggled – we giggled together – at the same time. Before we slept he told me about his twin sister. Who died. Of malaria. I could hear his voice crying when he said her name. Yemesi. In the morning when we woke, he asked me to call him Taiwo. So I did after that. It suited him better than Matthew. Matthew reminded me of *my* bed, not his.

We caught a bus to Hatton Park.

Walking.

'How can yer bear it? Living in that little room with a mouldy shower?'

'It's a step on my journey.'

'Where to?'

'To death?'

79

'God, that's not for ages yet.'

'Yes, but we pass through many things before we reach, and each step is a step closer.'

'Still. Don't see what living in a hovel has to do with it. Yer can't be that happy, no matter what yer say.'

'I'm happy. I know where I'm going. My grandfather . . . he told me that desire is destructive. That life is a passage, not a vessel. It cannot be filled. It can only be travelled. I can live in a palace or a hovel and be happy. I choose my way. I move my own clouds, when and if I need to. I don't measure my happiness by what I have, but by how I feel and how much I can give. Giving brings joy.'

'I don't get yer.'

'Do you believe in magic?'

'No. I hate it. I hate magicians anyway. Their funny clothes and rabbits and cards and . . . well, I think it's dead boring.'

'I have seen a man point with his finger to a bird in the sky and then watched it drop down on to the dirt, dead.'

'I don't think they'd like that sort of magic over here. They like seeing white birds flying out o' hats.'

'No. I'm talking about real magic. I can make clouds move. You could too.'

'Oh yeah. You'll 'ave me doin' a sun dance in a minute.'

'Lie down.'

In the park. Near the pond. Across from the weeping willow. He told me that clouds are easy. Less matter for the mind to govern. Less resistance. Clouds are easy.

I asked the clouds to move. My spirit gave its all to the task. There was just me. And the clouds. As soon as the clouds heard me, they moved. The sun hadn't been out all day but it came out for me. I thought about *Catweazle* and his elec-trickity. And I thought about my dad. And the sun blared then. In the glass of water that covered my eyes, I saw the bubbles again. I found myself in my eyes, in my freedom, in the skies.

When I wasn't looking at the skies I was looking at him. The people walked past us and thought we were family. The sun shone in the pond – back up to me. Reflections to feed me.

My picture was in the paper. I couldn't stop looking at it. They *must* be worried. I felt like I'd achieved something. I was only twelve in the picture. Now I was fifteen going on twenty-six. And strong. Taiwo's landlord saw the picture too and called the police who arrived just as we were tucking into spicy chicken and rice which we ate with our fingers.

'How long have you been here?'

'Did you come of your own free will?'

'Has this man done anything to you?'

Taiwo stood with his back straight, his fingers in the air, like he was in the middle of baking, the tomato sauce dripping on his feet, on the nail of his big toe.

'He's my friend.'

Taiwo bent down so I could kiss him on the cheek. I told him to carry on eating. Said it was important for him to eat.

The police took me home. Up the path. The roses were out (Blue Moon) in my dad's garden. The daffodils dead and gone. And I ran up the stairs without looking up. I don't know who opened the front door. In my room I looked at my face in the princess's mirror.

81

I felt like a princess then. For the first time since I was six.

Gary came in. Glaring at me. I reared up at him. His neck in my face. His thick neck. I screamed at it.

'Go on then. Hit me. Hit me, you bastard!'

With everything I had. He just stood there taking it. I slapped him about the face and pummelled at his stomach. His hard stomach. I wanted him to kill me. To do it to me. I wanted to be so crippled that my punishment cup would be full. But he just stood and took it. Crying. Not sobbing. Just trickles.

I could hear her. On the stairs. Coming up. Slow. Not sure. She was hesitating. She was going through the motions but she didn't know the racket waiting for her. She wasn't sure about this one. This one wasn't my fault. This one was her fault. It was all her fault.

'And you!' I pointed at her. 'You. I hate you. I hate you so much you'll never . . .'

Gary grabbed my pointing arm like the kung fu man. I spat at him. Well . . . I spat up at him but the pressure was pitiful. All the spit went down my jumper. She was hiding behind him. Like he was all she had left.

Then he whacked me round the back of the head. My mum stood in front of him. To stop him getting me again. I noticed her belly wasn't round and smooth. But it wasn't the belt she was carrying. She saw me looking. She stuck her hand into the pocket of her pinny and brought out the two little books. My diaries. Two whole years of mindless filth. She held them as a cross to Satan.

The next day they all went out. They didn't leave a note.

And from then on I was on my own. Even the bed felt

82

foreign. When they came back she came up to my room to tell me that everything I felt was true. I *was* foreign. I *was* on my own. She came up the stairs on nimble feet. Surprisingly.

'We've been to see the Canon.'

She was going through the motions. It was all over. She'd done her best. They were too old for any more trouble.

'He seems to think it'd be better for yer to go to a new family. He's had a look at the police report. That was enough for him. There was no need to show him the rest of the filth.'

She could see I was facing her out. Not a trace of a tear or fear crossed my face.

'I hope you're not pregnant, young lady, for your sake.'

She said that just to put the shits up me coz I was facing her with bare-faced cheek. And didn't care any more.

'He's sending someone to get you. A nun. She's called Sister Josephine. She'll pick yer up on Monday. Yer can try out a new place. See how they crack on with yer. We can't take much more of it. We can't . . .'

My head fell back on my pillow. Staring at the sky of my ceiling, under my breath, I said, 'Thank you, Taiwo – the cloud-mover.'

Sister Josephine, get yer skates on.

PART II

Chapter 11

'Have you had any thoughts on what job you're going to do?'

I was waiting for my dole cheque to slot through the letter box. It wasn't due for three days. I was sitting in *her* chair, the one with arms on, watching the telly. She was in my face, my space. That was her prerogative. It was her house. She sat on a hard chair and waved an envelope at me. I focused more intently on the television. Then to make her madder I punched at the buttons to change the channel. It was an Elvis anniversary.

'Have you had any thoughts on what job you're going to do?'

I never really liked Elvis. He was too Rock 'n' Rolly and I hated his hair. I knew she liked him so I drew her attention.

'Look!' I said. 'Elvis! All his films'll be on . . . Look!'

'I said have you had any thoughts on what job you're going to do. I need an answer.' She was well stroppy.

'Nothin',' under my breath.

Then I said it to her face. 'Nothin'.'

I studied the cabinet underneath the telly. Walnut stain.

Brass handles. Two drawer handles missing. Top drawer rubbish drawer. Curtain hooks. Shelled pens. Buttons. Letters.

'Well, I've taken the liberty of making some enquiries and I've managed to get you an interview.'

I eyed the envelope.

'At the hospital. They still have training places for nurses.'

I wanted to be a nurse like I wanted to be a fireman.

Mrs Wallace waved the brochure at me. I could see groups of nurses on it. Laughing across the front cover. I grabbed it and scanned the blurb without reading it. I stuffed it in the rubbish drawer and carried on watching the telly. She gathered her bulk and toppled into the kitchen. I could swear she was laughing. Check.

Give her her due. She'd tried.

When I saw her on the doorstep on the very first day, I knew. I knew then – it wouldn't work. She was waving . . . and Mr Wallace, he was there too, waving when I got out of the car. I didn't want a family that waved. Not when I was in spitting distance. Sister Josephine must have known that too. She'd been chatting with me all the way there. She was the one the rescue people sent out rescuing. Not talking, like Wilcox. She actually *did* the rescuing. Usually that meant taxi-ing kids from one unsuccessful home to another. That's what she told me. She must have known I didn't want a family that waved like that – but she left me there anyway. And left Mrs Wallace to get on with me. I wasn't easy. She put up with me for two years. She was good enough to wait for me to finish my education. I'll say that for her. She said it to me.

The school they sent me to was like the last but twice as. More nuns, kids, teachers, rules. More noise. More expected. More posh.

I tried to be good at first. Give myself a new start. Fresh start. Clean start. But the teachers turned out the same but twice as. Soppy, strict, posh, nasty. Clean and white and nice. They gave out books and talks and opinions. They had clean hands and medallions. And soon enough they despised me as the others had done. They ousted me from class as the others had done. I failed tests and they seethed over me as the others had done. I stood for hours in glass corridors, watching nuns hold hands with prep school shoots in the grasses, grasses that were strangled by glass, squared off away from the trees and the birds. I spent hours snatching squares of grey sky. Watching rain find the drainpipes. Leaves finding resting places down gulleys, for there was no free run. Not even for a leaf.

I saw quite a lot of Mother Superior's room. I studied her fancies, her tiny glass cats. Coloured boxes of paper handkerchiefs wearing woolly crocheted coats. Ink pens for men. Books about Rome and Roman buildings. Velvet pin cushions. What could she want with so many pins? To hold the white head-dress of supremacy together, in place. It never looked right. So there were hair grips as well. She had a passion for hair grips. Christ's passion each time she stuck them round the back of her neck, round her ears, which were massive and got in the way, lifting her head-dress, screwing up her face in pain, keeping the grey hairs inside the white hat. Like a child playing a continual game. Saw yer hair! Saw yer hair. Saw it! Saw it! First one caught showing any of their hair is Out Out Out . . . Why? For God's sake? I'm sure he wasn't bothered really. Or was it more the Benson and Hedges of nunnery. Habit. Fix head-dress. Habit. Wash hands, wash hands, wash hands. Fag, fag, fag. White Mother Superior.

They couldn't have been missionaries. Just me, me in school uniform, made them fidget. Not me in war paint, tribal etchings on my face, across my breasts, chanting round a bonfire, cauldron full of blood of white man. Me in school uniform. A shortage of black human landscape to practise on.

The civvy teachers were the worst. I exercised their charity above and beyond. After all they were teachers, not servants of the Lord. But God bless 'em.

'Could yer close yer legs, Miss Range, yer breath smells.'

Miss Range unbalanced, unfocused, ambushed and pounced on. Miss Range, needing glasses, hunting for her honour – on the desk, the floor, in the air above my head. I wasn't going to spend two years avoiding the flash of her crutch, seeing her flop flesh of thigh across a chair, distinguishing pubic hair. She could have sat behind the desk, not in front, trying to be with us, trying to make us feel her.

'Get your arse out of my face, Miss Range,' I could have said. I tried to be funny.

'She always sits like that,' they said.

They had a name for her. A really dirty name. She kept her legs crossed after what I said. The name no longer fitted. So it wasn't used. I did her a favour.

I was sent to the school dogs and savaged for that. The staff-room pack came out snapping back, personal. Vile. Just like me. Like I already was. Like I had already become. I learned to leather my skin against their assaults so they could not draw blood. They lived cosy lives in leafy suburbs and I rushed in and scorched them with my jungle sun. Scorched them so hot they could not teach me A levels or diplomacy. They wrote, 'Insolent, vindictive, common and foul-mouthed' behind the ticks and crosses on my workbook, when and if it landed on their dining-room table, after dinner was done and the kids were in bed and the husband was slumped and whiskied in front of the telly.

Parents? I dithered on calling them Aunty and Uncle for ages. For ages nothing. I ruled out first names. I couldn't call a grown-up by their first name. Still. I settled on Mr and Mrs Wallace. Like they were landlord and lady, which is what they were. The service was crap and the food worse. After just three months of soaring costs, my benefactors began to despise me. They had one more of my sort, Linzi. She came from a Catholic orphanage in Liverpool which she said was rammed to the gills with half-caste disposables waiting and wanting to be recycled. She was fourteen and beginning to rebel. I helped her on her way. She lost her 'proper' virginity before I did. But I didn't tell her that. I wouldn't have heard the end of it.

My girlfriends started doing things like UCCA and Oxbridge and clearing houses and grades and taking mocks seriously. They talked about going to places like York and Bath, Lancaster and London, Leeds and Brighton. They were grown-up. They were going away to find fancy husbands but, if the worst came to the worst, they could get a degree. I went to bed and scratched my arms with a compass till they bled. Confirmation that I was still alive. Instead of crying.

Mrs Wallace paid for me to go out because I made trouble else. I could gee up Linzi like a babe before bedtime, getting her hot and dizzy with anger, red-eared with ruddy romping. Or I'd have friends come over, clonking around in the bedroom, drinking orange, milk, coffee, beer. Populating the bathroom in twos and threes, washing hair and blowing dryers, perfuming the towels and leaving cotton-wool trails up and down the stairs like whores at a cabaret.

Mr Wallace didn't come up and say anything. He didn't want to show us his wah-wah. He lived in his own room and we never saw him or his big colour telly or his stereo system that he part-exchanged every year for the latest model. Or his special food which he kept locked in a cupboard. He had a big lump on his head. That was his wah-wah. In the end we all called him Wah-wah. He wrote to the Pope a lot and played chess. I don't know if he ever wrote back. And he translated theological papers into Greek. When I first arrived, he said he'd like to teach me Greek. With a big smile on his face, his wah-wah bobbin' about on his forehead. I just humoured him. Said I couldn't wait like . . .

Mrs Wallace was too embarrassed to show us her distress. She couldn't raise a voice or a teenager. The music, loud and repetitive, gave the house to me. The Wallaces sat downstairs waiting for us girls upstairs to get tired. Like we were drunken landowners and they the house servants.

When I received my first dole cheque I went to the pictures, then to the pub and on to a night-club. Then I sat and watched telly and waited for the next one.

But that was it. Once the dole cheques started rolling in she got busy. I had a feeling she'd been up to something.

The morning of the nursing interview I dressed in black but decided on saving the make-up palaver for the bus ride. No way was I going to be a nurse. Mrs Wallace would have to go back to the drawing board. My plan was to get the bus fare off her and sod off somewhere else for the day.

I put on my sickly smile and headed towards her in the kitchen. Her black cardigan dazzled gold bullion buttons at me. Her lipstick crunched as her mouth opened and closed like an overglossed door. She had one on as well – a sickly smile. Then it changed to a check-mate smile. She did king-size bobs right past me and got to her chair where her handbag was. I hoped to get my bus fare. Her hands were in there, in the bag, reaching for the purse. She pulled out the lipstick to re-apply. A gaze of victory tottered under her glasses, waiting to bob me right in the face.

'Oh, you won't be needing bus fare,' she said. Bob. Bob.

She was fat, about sixteen stone. She ate better than she fed us. Us being Linzi and me. She fed us on mash nearly every day. Not because that's what we wanted but because she couldn't go wrong with mash. Mash and sausages. Mash and beans. Mash and fried eggs. She had an egg-frying pan which she never emptied. She just added more and more fat to it. When she fried eggs in it they blew up like bombs in her face. They came out sauce brown with black bits all over. She did eggs like that on Sundays after Mass and Benediction.

'You won't be needing bus fare because I'm coming with you.'

Gloves on. Too small. Made her hands look deformed. Bulging stretched knuckles and empty tips. Teats of a black lamb to pay the bus conductor with. She might take the gloves off. She doesn't need gloves. It's August. They'll laugh at her. People like her don't catch buses to Liverpool. They go to Chester in cars.

'Why yer comin' with me? I don't need my hand holdin'. I know how to get there.'

'Because I want to.'

We never spoke all the way.

I went into the interview alone. Biology was compulsory, it said so on the blurb. I didn't have biology. I failed the exam twice. I pointed this out to the man. There was just one man.

'Doesn't matter,' he says. 'Your two A levels more than make up for that.'

'Classical Civilization isn't what I'd call a good groundin' . . . as it says in the blurb.'

'On the contrary.' He smiled.

His eyes were giddy. His fingers neat and nails well cared for. He looked like he was moulded to the desk and if he stood up the desk would be stuck to his tie.

He crossed the 'T's, tidied his papers, stacked them square and dotted the 'I's.

My name fell – the last to fill a mass grave – to the bottom of his list.

'Would you like to ask your guardian to come in now?'

The conspiracy unwrapped like the final act of a shit play. She came in grinning. They shook hands and congratulated one another. I had six days left of not being a nurse.

Game over.

The night before I left that childhood, I went for a goodbye

94

drink, got drunk all night and never slept a wink. Never made it home either. I skulked back the following morning . . . to a note:

We have gone to Blackpool for the day. Your suitcase is on the landing, packed. Your room has been cleared. Malcolm from St Teresa's will call round at 11 a.m. to take you to the hospital. Good Luck!
Mr and Mrs Wallace

There was some charity in that. It was well thought out. It was non-compromisory. It fitted the event. It was non-loving. Non-hostile. It was nothing but 'Good Luck'. I was glad to be spared any false farewells. Linzi. I thought *she* might have left a note. And who the friggin' hell was Malcolm?

It made me think of when I left the Milners. They did their goodbyes like I was going on holiday. 'Got everything?' 'Praps yer better tie that suitcase with some string in case it bursts open.' Stuff like that. After the bags and the cases were packed in the boot and I was sat in the passenger seat, they stood by the gate with their arms folded. Mum and Dad. Stood with their arms folded and then when the car started moving, they lifted one of their folded arms and did a wave with it, the other arm still folded. As I say, like I was going on holiday.

At the hospital, a woman who called herself 'the warden' searched up and down a clipboard list of names. She couldn't find mine.

'Could yer spell it?' She was Irish. She was looking at me like I'd just got off a boat.

'M I L N E R . . . how it sounds.'

Then I had a thought. Mrs Wallace had done all the paper work. Maybe they had me down as Wallace. She looked but there wasn't a Wallace on the list either. She went into her office and shut the door . . . in my face. I heard the ding of a telephone. When she came out everything was fine. Follow her. Eventually we arrived at my room. She searched her bunch of keys for the right one and let us in. Malcolm and me. There was just enough space to walk round the drawers, bed, wardrobe and desk. She asked me for a £1.75 deposit for the key. I looked at Malcolm. He looked like a geography teacher – lost. No map.

The warden just stood there with her hand out.

Malcolm paid her and then gave me the change from a five-pound note. He escaped after that in case someone thought he was my dad.

I still felt drunk from the night before.

Chapter 12

After the door on my history closed leaving me rattling around in my future, I paused for breath. A deep breath. Then I opened my suitcase to bring out familiarity. Add something to the sterility. On top of the clothes and the plastic bags was an envelope.

Ahh! Here's the real note, I thought.

I sat in that room alone. Truly alone. I was used to conflict. My verbal skills were fashioned and honed on dealing with conflict. For the first time in my life, it dawned on me that I was so good at living and dealing out conflict I'd cleared the battlefield. All the enemies were gone. The note. The envelope. In there would be the chance to re-establish a battleground. Whilst I was opening the envelope I had already decided to write and say sorry. A promise to act more maturely. Not to engage in battle at every given opportunity.

The paper was cream-coloured like my O level certificates. It was a certificate of some sort, I could tell. I tried to slide it out of the envelope without creasing the paper. I turned it over. It was my birth certificate.

O'Leary. Mary O'Leary. Name of Father – Blank.

Name of Child – Josephine. Occupation of mother – student.

The blank bugged me. More than the Mary. I was Josephine O'Leary. And the invisible mother had a name. An Irish name.

I went to tell the warden that I was Josephine O'Leary so she could tick me off her list.

She knew, she said. She already *had* ticked me off her list. Without batting an eyelid.

Then there were three days of near starvation. Memories of speckled bombed eggs. Three days of mouth dry tobaccoed tastelessness. Of salt 'n' vinegar crisps for breakfast, dinner and tea. Stinging the ribbed roof of my mouth and making the raw walls of my cheeks scream. Of sucking potato till its acid sting fell to my belly neutralised leaving soggy nuggets to rest in clattering cavities. Filling cavities but not belly or soul.

Three nights of walking the streets like a part-time tramp, waiting for the girls, the little nursies, to finish cooking and eating their menu-planned tea. It took them that many days to wonder where the girl from Room 44 grubbed up. Of conflict ebbing on a tide of silence. I baited the waters, half speaking when spoken to. Three days of my earth-root pride versus the innocence of their curiosity which, with each day that passed, cooked and browned off to a snubbed indifference.

Eight o'clock was usually late enough for me to slink back into the nurses' home undetected by the new recruits. By that time, in the kitchen, their sweet white wine was warming along with their sweet conversation.

I sneaked up the stairways on my return, to snatch

remnants of a life story floating out of the kitchen along with the smell of a sizzling pork chop. Tiptoeing past I ate that smell for sustenance, for to promise myself that chop or toasted teacake, the very same bacon and egg. I heard them say things like, 'It's my little sister's birthday on Saturday. I think I'll get her a nurse's outfit.'

Stuff like that.

Once in my room I flopped down on the bed and waited again. I waited till there was a lull in their mood, until their conversation hummed like a trapped bee in the airy corridors – anonymous corridors of doors and doors. White. Then I got up and shook myself and took a casual wander to the kitchen with my hands in my back pockets and a grin from ear to ear. I asked them questions about that day's lessons. I gave them frank and false synopses of what I thought about the teachers, the content, the uniform. It was the 'Be positive', 'Stiff upper lip', 'Give it time' – waste of bloody time convention. After a cup of water, drunk in sips, stood at the sink, piled high with clean plates, shiny from the anxious scrubs of carefully brought-up children, I said my good-nights. With my hands back in pockets, I hummed my way down the corridor to my room. In there I splashed my face at the sink, for to believe myself, for to believe my life.

On the fourth day, after my whorey stroll round telephone-box street corners, past shops of small men and fat old women, I came back to find, on the desk in my room, a plate covered over with a pan lid. And a knife and fork. I lifted the lid to find mashed potatoes, mince and peas. I sat down to the supper like a muppet. At last fed. As a matter of *fact* I had to eat. My stomach swelled at the shock and begged for no more. My head was pissed off. I'd been got at. They had conspired to feed me. Which meant that they were talking about me. They had been in my room, seen the paint torn away by the posters of the girl who lived there before me. Seen the electric-plug sockets empty of anything electric. The unmade bed, the overflowing ashtray, the blood-stained knickers soaking in the sink. After the last warm mouthful I could manage, I sat scared. I was too scared to go and face the cooks. The cooks were waiting – I could hear their chairs scraping against the kitchen floor – but no hum, no screeches of delight and laughter, the getting-to-know-you-quite-well safety of their laughter. My gratitude suspended. Their compassion ignored. It was the first time I'd ever felt scared for myself. For my next move. For my very being.

The very first afternoon I went mad and bought fags, some mags and Sunday newspapers. I didn't speak to a soul. I settled down to a night alone with the newspapers. I couldn't read past the third page. I spent more time reading and re-reading my birth certificate. My room beckoned attention, at every rattle of the page in emptiness. I looked but saw nothing. I strained and heard nothing. I lay back and day-dreamed running wild. I was wild. Nobody knew me or of me. There was a white-walled world out there not yet contaminated by me. Not yet full and overdone. I asked my grown-up self for help.

Out loud.

'Josephine O'Leary. Help me to make things go OK.'

Then I fell asleep.

In the morning a knock at the door woke me up. I opened the door slightly ajar. A woman stood there, grey hair, jangling keys. Another warden. She wore her white uniform like a nurse and her face like a mistake.

'Time to get up,' she snarled. 'You're late.'

She shut the door for me. Took it out of my hand. Like it was *her* door.

I stared out of the window, at the mean lump of sky open to me, to other windows the same as mine. All the windows were the same, broken into nine oblongs. I looked at my nine windows, and noticed the bottom window-frames cleaner than the top. At the top, a fly bungled his way into a spider trap. The trap was only half a circle, the other half demolished or maybe not yet built. I took a piece of newspaper, screwed it up, climbed on to the windowsill and killed both the fly and the spider by pulverising them with my covered fist. The sun peeped into my rationed sky.

I went to the wrong place first off. I saw half a sign, the half that said 'school'. I followed the trail down a ramp to a beautiful Georgian house that looked like it was put there by accident, amidst the architectural mistakes of the fifties. It was the school for doctors. It reminded me of my old convent school. It had mock Corinthian columns with a frieze across depicting a baby being held up by a man with a beard. At first I thought the baby was Jesus but I wondered . . . there were naked people dancing about. It was probably a sacrifice to the goddess who was showing one breast and doing a fireman's slide down one of the central columns. A Doric column? I tried hard to remember my columns. She couldn't have been Mary. What with the breast . . . and she was eyeing up the baby like she wanted to eat it.

A jobsworth wearing an *On-the-Buses* uniform put me

101

right. He directed me to the nursing school. I walked under a bridge. It seemed to join the nurses' home to the hospital. Green and yellow corrugated plastic. I could see nurses burrowing their way along it to the wards. Like tiny maggots. Beneath it cars flew past on a dual carriageway. I walked past an old man wearing a cap, stood at the bus stop holding a big black bin bag to his chest. He was crying. I wondered what was in the bag. Later on I'd learn. It was his wife. Or what was left of her.

Then I came to the school. This was a flat grey building modelled on a giant prefab. In the reception, two women, both with glasses, eyed me. They were waiting for me, they said. One was holding a kettle. She dropped it to take down my details. I saw my name towards the end of her typed list of new recruits. Josephine O'Leary. I found the way to the classroom by myself so they could have their tea.

They were all sat at desks in couplets. There was one empty desk next to a Chinese girl. Nobody sat next to her because she was foreign, I reckoned. She never smiled when I walked towards her. I felt the eyes of the class giving me a good going over so I turned my head round really quick – exorcist-style – to catch them at it, to let them know I wasn't going to stand any nonsense. One of them giggled. I think it was Sylvie.

We soaked up new vocabulary as we skipped from ward to ward on the blackboard floor plan of the hospital. We were given lots of forms to fill in and asked to pay £15 to go on some register. Within seconds everyone was writing cheques. Unbelievable.

'Who hasn't paid?'

No one put their hand up but a few of them dared to look at me.

At break time someone told me that pay day was the end of the month.

Twenty-four days to go.

On the second day we prepared for our first hospital visit. We were given new white uniforms with our names, O'Leary, blood red embroidered in the collar. The cape was the best. That had my O'Leary in it too. It was bright red teddy-bear soft inside and navy blue out. There were two thick red bands that tied over the breasts to draw a large red ready-for-action cross against the white uniform. I let the body of the cape billow and swallow me up and then ran like the wind Batman-ing all the way back to the nurses' home.

We were given a sheet of white cardboard. It was in the shape of a polygon. Every time my maths teacher drew a polygon it was always the same shape. The cardboard was this shape. We were asked to turn it into a hat. Origami. I wasn't keen. I let the Chinese girl do mine. She'd be a dab hand at it, I reckoned. The white hat had a thick green stripe going across it. This indicated that I was a first-year student nurse. Not a lowlier pupil nurse with a yellow stripe or a rock-bottom auxiliary with no stripes at all.

The hats were for telling who could tell who what to do. They weren't anything to do with hygiene! And not much bigger than an empty bog roll anyway.

When I put my hat on, I couldn't see the green stripe. My Afro was so wide, I could barely see the hat.

All the nurses had little watches hanging out of their breast pockets. They were all comparing like with like. Some had had them engraved – 'To Sandra – Nurse Thorn – Mitton Hospital, Love Mum and Dad'. Sick. They wore a regulation moccasin shoe, black or brown. There was a picture of the shoe, badly drawn, in the induction booklet. It was a relief to see it in its true form. I wore pumps. I thought my pumps were really clean until I put on the Daz dress they called a uniform. I wore black tights with a ladder up the inside leg. It was on the outside leg really but I'd twisted the tights round to make it the inside. I saw some nail varnish in the bathroom at the nurses' home and used it to splodge the ladder to stop it running. A big pink splodge.

Everyone else was shipshape, all present and correct. Hair brushed to death. Stinking of perfume. Blasé and Youth Dew.

As we walked through the hospital grounds other nurses gave us the once-over. The sneer. The giggle. They had two or three stripes, some of them. We were straight out of a toy shop. Shiny and new. Red crosses emblazoned across our chests like soldiers without drums. None of the real nurses sported red crosses and slowly we loosened our straps so's not to look quite so stupid.

We all had a death wish – to be the first to see a dead body. But we were reverent. Clutching our capes as virgins. Talking in whispers. The tutor led us to the hospital with a quick step. At the entrance to the ward we were stopped and silenced. I was looking for a font of holy water to douse myself a sign of the cross.

The patients were men suffering from bad coughs, strokes and heart attacks. Some were in bed and some out. Others sad and others who looked as fit as a fiddle. There were men breathing through transparent plastic masks with steam coming out of the side. Tall black oxygen tanks, like war

104

relics, stood next to their beds. Diabetics and epileptics sparkled youth.

I watched the nurses. They were walking really quickly with bottles or really slowly with drips on wheels. They swung curtains round beds and then dived inside to do things. What were they doing in there? Sometimes they were in there for ages. They filled in numbers on charts, moved tables and shook thermometer sticks. And smiled. I didn't see much to grin at.

There was a nurse in a dark-blue uniform with blue stripes on her hat. Sister. She had a red cord dangling from a navy-blue belt wrapped round a neat waist. Only trained nurses could wear belts. It was all a bit like judo really.

On the end of the red cord was the in-charge key.

'Whenever you go on a ward, look for the nurse with the red cord. It might be round her neck, dangling outside her pockets or (as Sister's was) dangling from the belt. This is the nurse in charge.'

Forget all about judo belts and lines round a hat.

Sister was a typical matron. Buxom and fierce. She was tall. She could take a knock. Thick arms, fast legs, hair fierce behind her cap, eyes scurrilously searching for a fragment of pretension or sycophancy. Heat waves melting the air round an engine, nurses swam round her, never to her.

'Who are Smethers, O'Leary and Ravencroft?'

I was as dazed as the patients. The only hospital I'd ever seen was on the telly. The full smack of the trick that got me into that hospital ward made my eyes sting. I didn't recognise my name. Of course, O'Leary. That was me. I shot my hand up late.

'Are we keeping you awake, Nurse O'Leary?' Sister didn't like me, I could tell. Nurse O'Leary. One of the boy nurses was Smethers and Ravencroft was Sylvie.

'Well, you lucky three will be working this ward. With me. I have your allocation sheet here.' She was waving it about like it was our execution warrant.

'You'll have plenty to do here – so enjoy school whilst you can.'

With that she was gone. As I caught my breath, my balance, she turned around. Roared her engine again. Dragon.

'Sorry, I can't come with you. Consultant's round any minute. Good luck.'

Then a dirty laugh which gave me hot ears. Her name was Sister Bleek.

And then back to the patients. Hidden in chairs. Under bedclothes. Behind curtains. Slunk over tables. Sleeping. Behind masks. The younger ones were animated and talking to each other. They looked healthy and stupid wearing pyjamas in broad daylight.

They looked at *us* with a measure of awe, unaware of the kicks and punches we were learning to deliver them. These men thought we were nurses. None of us spoke up and told the truth. We walked around the ward as actresses at a dress rehearsal. I couldn't look them in the eye.

After a visit to the bathroom where I caught sight of an old man with only one foot being chair-lifted into the bath, *I* felt like the victim. I was surrounded by pain and suffering but *I* felt like the victim.

'Now, nurses – let's go back and join the other group.'

Chapter 13

I wanted courage. Courage to go to the nursies in the kitchen and say 'Thank you'. But I didn't know who to. Who fed me? They were waiting.

I wanted to be a performing clown playing for laughs that are thrown in the air for me to catch in a basket and then wrap myself up, in my bed, teddy bears of applause and loyalty, sleeping in white cotton care. They were waiting.

There was a knock at my door. A small nurse in uniform but no hat. Gravy down her front. Long hair and a fresh complexion. She was grinning nervously. She was Sylvie. She opened her mouth to speak but I stole her place and jumped in her face grabbing the opportunity for myself. Before any more kindness could be forced upon me.

'Thanks for my dinner. That was really kind. Thank you.'

Her mouth closed automatically – like a machine shutting off. She waited until the silence stretched before opening it again. So she was sure of delivery. I wondered whether her speech was rehearsed. Had they all been sitting in the kitchen composing it and then taken a vote on who would deliver it?

She rowed on my outburst with a competent paddle, sure of her voice in a flow, as though she could take the conversation wherever I wanted to go, up to a pressure point or down to a murmuring simmering slow.

'Why didn't you say somethin', divvy? We wondered why we never saw you eat anything or cook anything. You should have said something.'

She was looking over my shoulder at the plate. It was an embarrassing plate. I danced to the side to hide it.

'Well, yer can't go asking people yer don't know for food, can yer? I didn't know what to do.'

'Go and get a sub.'

'What's a sub?'

I let her in. She stood against the window burning her hands on the radiator. She seemed to like burning her hands. She kept flinching with pain and then putting her hands back on the hot metal. She didn't look at the plate. The day was still light but the room dim, which helped. She would be my friend. I'd known from day one.

'They give you money in advance of your wages. Go and ask them. I'm sure they'll do it. You can't live on nothing.'

'I will. I'll do it. I didn't know you could do stuff like that. Thanks.'

'Well, what d'yer think then . . . of the course? What d'yer think?'

''S OK.'

I didn't know how to carry on the conversation. I wanted to carry it on though. I would have stepped in front of her if she'd tried to get out. Another night alone might have pushed me over some edge that didn't look like it had a trampoline landing.

'I hate it,' she said.

'So do I.'

'D'yer wanna go for a walk? 'Ave a look round the area?'

After ten minutes of walking, the autumn trying light gave way to a warning winter dark. We both turned and smiled at exactly the same time. There were black clouds threatening the early stars above and the council houses were lit up like bigger stronger stars waving to the baby ones who were going to die in the cloud. I wanted to live in the stars, the earth stars. I wanted to be in those bathrooms, living rooms, bedrooms. I wanted someone to come out of one of the houses and wave at me shouting and laughing, excited at my good fortune, arms open and welcoming, saying, 'This is your house. You can have it. We've been waiting for you . . .'

Sylvie pulled me in off the road – I was walking aimlessly into the traffic, my mind away with relaxing.

My brain woke up.

'Come-ed. I quickened the pace. 'Hey, yesterday I noticed a gate down 'ere that said "Private". It's a park or somat. We could get inside and see what's in there.'

That was a test. Was she a divvy? Would she protest? She did not. She followed floppy soft as a puppy. She was agile climbing the gate. She had a huge backside and huge tits but the rest of her was thin. An unfortunate shape. I wasn't slim but I was in proportion. Big all over.

'So why Mitton Hospital?' she asked me. 'Why d'yer come 'ere?'

We were snaking around a path that was bordered with leather leaves shining mustard from the street light. A winter blow got into autumn and made a paper bag of my bomber jacket. Sylvie wore a donkey jacket. Flushed and fiery, her cheeks warmed me and her smile was the softest thing I'd felt for days.

'I dunno. It was all organised for me really. Hey, let's go this way. Look! There's another path over 'ere. C'mon!'

'Who organised it for you? Your mum and dad?'

'Yeah, sort of. I don't really wanna talk about it. Why did *you* come 'ere? It's fuckin' crap.'

'Well, I failed my A levels. All of 'em. I couldn't think of anything else to do and I wanted to help people.'

'Yer sound like Miss fuckin' World. D'yer think you'll like it?'

I was swearing out of relaxing. I hadn't sworn for days and days. Like food. I was starved of speaking the words I was used to. I wanted to swear so much my conversation was chucking up on it.

'Dunno. Don't 'ave much choice.'

I understood that.

We picked our way down the narrowing path, dark, overgrown with plants, worryingly alive. A man with a sharp stick stabbed me in the shin. I shrieked in horror. Sylvie turned to save me from my unknown assailant and we both fell about laughing. We could only just make out the guilty bush. It was true dark. It was true silent when we stood still. Surrounded by foliage we felt lost and lusty for more adventure. The path ended. Shhhhhh! My fingers on my lips. A bird joined in the fun, slapping the night with his wing machine and laughing after our fright.

A barrier of sleeping sunflowers six foot high stared down at us.

'Shall we go back?' Sylvie whispered.

'Scaredy babby. Course not. We're 'ere now.'

'Just testin',' she said.

I liked her a lot. We began to pick our way through the sunflowers. They mooned down on us, their faces teasing us, their hair wet and wilted. When we could see nothing but sunflowers all around us and the clouds had wiped the stars out for good and the silence screamed as we swept stems out of our way, we were really scared. My blood was warm and pumping. At last. I knew I was all right. I hadn't changed. I thought the 'me' inside had died. But I was back with a vengeance, trespassing in the black night of a strange land. We were only a mile away from the nurses' home – if that. It didn't matter. I needed a new land of my own, a place to find me in. And this was it. I ran through the sunflowers in triumph, thumping them as I leapt as though they were my enemy. Sylvie ran behind laughing and pushing me and we both howled with dare.

Eventually, a clearing and a building, tall with high long windows like those of a church. It wasn't a church. We could see neon lights inside, hanging from tall ceilings on sticks. We could hear strange noises. They were human noises but unintelligible.

'Give us a leg up and I'll have a look inside.'

I didn't want to. I wanted to be first, but Sylvie was right, she weighed less than me.

'Well, let me see after then?' I eyed her with some contempt.

'I'll try. C'mon. Let me up.' I cupped my hand and strained to lift her as high as I could. I wanted her to feel how strong I was. She shot up like a rocket. She was very light.

'What is it? What's in there?'

111

She jumped off me, scraping her hand against the wall. After examining her wound, and making me mad with suspense, she eventually looked at me disgusted.

'Have a look.'

She cupped her hands for me. I put my muddy pumped foot in it, heaving myself up to headbutt the wall. She couldn't lift a ten-pound bag of spuds. I showed her how to do it properly. She was better the next time but I was only able to grab about three seconds before I had to jump down and escape serious injury.

'Fuckin"ell,' was all I could say. My head hurt. I felt it for blood. I was eight years old.

Inside the building was a ward of a hospital. Most of the beds were empty. Men were walking around, some half dressed, others lying down on the floor. Grown men walking round sucking their thumbs. We'd broken into a loony bin.

The silence of indecision went on too long.

'Let's get out of here.'

We both ran in mad bounds like mad hounds creating more panic to add to the excitement. Bashing and shrieking our way through the sunflowers, we eventually got back to the gate. We gasped for ages and laughed like drunkards before we climbed back over.

'Shall we go for a drink?'

'Can't. I'm skint, remember.'

'I'll get 'em in. I'll lend yer some money. You'll be all right when you get a sub.'

'All right then.'

I was feeling great. I was getting my bearings. As we walked, I looked at her from the side and saw how careless she was. She wasn't having any difficulty with silence. She didn't talk shit for shit's sake. She caught me looking and smiled.

We got to the pub that sat next to the hospital. The Red Horse. In the bright light, the leaves and shrubbery grew on us. Sylvie knocked a few leaves from my Afro and I did likewise to her hair. We laughed. Loads of people were staring at us. In one corner of the pub there was a circle of young men all loud crowded up on one another. They sported jars of ale and tipped them down their necks in a sort of frenzy and then sat back and laughed. They were the heart of the pub and everyone else mere corpuscles carrying oxygen of publicity to make them laugh louder. We stole their oxygen for a minute or two.

We bought a couple of half-lagers and blackcurrant, and sat with the gang of men on our left where we could see them. Sylvie didn't pay any attention to them. I did. They were easily spottable as young doctors. One looked at me like I was a new piece of furniture, just a hint of curiosity. I was the only black person there. I was always the only black person anywhere. I turned away in case he thought I fancied him.

Sylvie gave me the run-down on the girls that lived on our landing. There was Miriam, one A level, no boyfriend, boring. Sandra, engaged to a sailor, one A level, quick and clever but very moral. And Jackie. Quiet, engaged to a man who managed a group of butcher's shops. They were the central core of the landing. Other girls from upstairs were Jackie again, fat and funny, and Annabel, the daughter of a vicar. Inside I was disappointed as hell. Outside I feigned interest and delight. She really seemed to like them all.

After another couple of halves and long accounts of Chipper, her boyfriend, we went back to the home. Nobody

113

was around. There was a note from the nursies saying they'd gone to the television room. I didn't want to join them so I went to bed and left Sylvie friendless in the kitchen.

Back in my room, I went over what had happened. My room was beginning to take shape. The hat hung on the mirror above the sink, the cape on the back of the door. I was beginning to feel like a nurse. I felt stronger. The next day – maybe money. I could buy food and cook. I slept in this cocoon of hope.

I woke early and sat in bed smoking the last of my fags. There was no way of knowing time. I waited until I heard the girls shivering from showers down the corridor. I never had a shower because I didn't have a towel. There was a small hand towel in my room which I used for washing. It was getting grubby. My pants I had to scrub with the tiny bar of soap provided and that was nearly all gone. I had no shampoo or deodorant or even a toilet bag. I finished the last fag and set off for school early so I could find out about my sub.

By the time school started, the sub was all arranged and I had thirty pounds in my pocket. When the tutor drew a picture of a respiratory passage on the blackboard, I wanted out. How could I take it in? I wanted to go shopping. Then she started talking about emphysema, cancer, chronic bronchitis, pulmonary oedema, and I got interested again. The new words were put on the blackboard. The symptoms really interested me. Dry mouth, tachycardia, spoon-shaped fingers, swollen ankles, anxiety. I wanted to get back on the ward and see who had spoon-shaped fingers and blue extremities. It wasn't like proper school. I enjoyed quite a lot of the stuff they threw at us. Everybody else looked dazed by the onslaught. I loved it. I even put my hand up to answer a couple of the teacher's questions. That was a first. No one else knew the answer! I was tired of waiting for them.

Sylvie stayed cool. As she had done the days previously, she sat with the others, the Jackies and Sandras of this world.

At the end of break she just said, 'Did yer get yer sub?' I told her I'd pay her back later. She grinned.

At lunchtime, I bought a big ham batch, a yoghurt and a can of Coke. It was heaven. I bought twenty fags and nearly made myself sick smoking so many so fast. I bought a toilet bag, a bar of Lux soap, a loaf of bread, some potatoes, a lamb chop, a tin of peas, some soap powder, a newspaper, a pair of tights and a bath towel – huge and lovely. The shoes would have to wait for the weekend. I did my homework whilst they were still trying to explain to the class how to do it. At the end of the school day I was wishing I'd bought myself some butter and bubble bath.

That evening, I cooked with the rest of them. They were eating that Smash again. I cooked proper potatoes but had to ask if I could borrow some butter. They were all quiet. Sylvie went to see her boyfriend.

'Hey, have you done your homework?'

'Me?' I said, pointing to myself.

'Yeah, we wondered if you could help us.'

'Course I can. After tea, eh?'

'You don't mind, do yer?' This was Sandra. She looked a bit cocky. She didn't want to be asking.

'God no! Course not. Don't mind a bit.' And that was true. I really did want to help.

We all sat around the kitchen table with books. They all

had books. I pointed out as best I could what they should pay attention to and what to ignore. I gave them ways to help them remember things.

At the end of the week, a poster went up on the noticeboard. A jumble sale of nurses' books and clothing and miscellaneous was to be held on the Saturday. This was how all the trained nurses got rid of the stuff they didn't need. I bought my books, my watch, a metal hatpin and an old radio for less than five pounds. I was over the moon. I went to Liverpool and got myself a new pair of shoes. When I got back to the nurses' home, my joy dissolved. There was nobody there. I knew there wouldn't be but the emptiness of our long corridor sapped up my busy day and turned it into something to mock and ridicule. My little carrier bags of triumph turned into purchases of desperation. I got that trapped feeling again.

Sunday night, and slowly the new nursies returned, ready for another week. They had pictures to put on their walls, cards from their little sisters, tons of food and loads of chat. I was happy.

Chapter 14

I didn't like the way the landing went quiet every Friday night. The nursies waving their goodbyes with their heads to one side in pity and and a gladness sparkling in their eyes. Glad of their lives. I disappeared out of sight before they could do it to me. To the TV room. The TV room was a ghosted ballroom with a dangerous shiny parquet floor, remnantly carpeted, edged with second-hand couches. One Friday night I was joined by a male nurse from our class. Kevin. He only lived up the road, he said. He preferred staying at the nurses' home though. His parents were a pain. We went to the pub that night and arranged to spend our Saturday together.

Kevin was a weed. Looked like a drink of water. His hair was painted thin blond across an egg-shaped head and his glasses were grey and big. He didn't look much like a Scouser and to me Scousers look like Scousers. There's something in the lip-hang, the quick eye, the ease of expression. They grab sentences out of your mouth before you've even said 'em. Kevin had hardly any lip, was close to blind and blushed if he raised his voice past a whisper. He wasn't my sort at all but he was company.

We got on the bus around lunchtime. I said I wanted to go to the cathedral.

'Which one?' he asked.

'The cathedral.'

'There's two cathedrals. Didn't yer know that?'

I remembered the words of the song, 'If yer want a cathedral, we've got one to spare'. I should have known. I remembered going to the opening of Liverpool Cathedral with me mum and dad and half the church on a big long coach. We had ham butties that day. That was the big round cathedral. After the opening, we walked swamped in a crowd, for ages, in a great long line, shouting 'No to Abortion'. I didn't know that Liverpool already had a cathedral.

'Why did they build two?'

'One's for Catholics,' he said.

He took me to the other one. To convince me. He took me down through a door that said 'Private'. My favourite sort of door. It led to a cellar. He told me he used to hide out in the cellar when he was bunking from school.

'They never would have looked for me in enemy territory,' he said.

He called his school a seminary, which made me think of sperm, and him too, I think.

'What's a seminary?'

'I hated it,' he answered, not answering, talking to himself.

We both sat on a pew with a broken leg but holding up easily on the fractured wood. They don't make 'em like that any more, we joked. It was leaning against a wall. The light bulb swung, *Callan*-style. We lit up. Kevin relaxed and sat on the floor instead. He was re-living his schooldays, dragging hard on his fag and blowing smoke rings to the glare of the bulb. I gave that up in fourth year. I rocked the pew in boredom hoping it would break and cause a clatter. I wanted to scream really. He started talking like he was making his first confession, all wimpy but getting stronger as the sins fell out, like the way water goes down a plug hole.

'The priests were really hypocritical. They used to bugger half the kids. Some 'ad prostitutes in at night. We could hear their 'igh 'eels runnin' along the corridor. One of the priests tried to get me once. I shit myself but I got 'im off me.'

He stumped his fag out on the pew, burning the wood, twisting it in, just to burn the wood good.

'Some of them were all right but loads weren't. Me dad, it was. He made me go. I was there for nearly five years. Learning to be a priest. Just for him. I couldn't stand it.'

He got up smiling. His confession over. I followed him out. He stopped me turning the light switch off. I guess he wanted someone to know we'd been. Maybe that someone might think God had been. Then I remembered that God didn't smoke.

'God, I never realised that boys went to priest school. I went to a convent but they didn't train us to be nuns. Yer could go for it if you 'ad the calling like, but none of us did. Did you ever think you 'ad the calling?'

'Yeah, sometimes. Sometimes when the choir sang in tune. When the sun came through the stained-glass windows and it was my turn to dress the priest and his robes turned all coloured with reds and yellows and purples and he looked like he was decked out in jelly babies. Sometimes it felt like God wanted me.'

'And what made you think he didn't?'

'When I woke up in the morning and thought: I fuckin'
'ate God, I fuckin' 'ate 'im. I knew priests weren't s'posed
to think like that. We had to go to Mass at six and do
Bible at seven and who the fuck wants to do that unless
yer gonna be a priest. I knew I wasn't a proper priest. I
knew I wasn't queer either and I 'ated what they did to
the boys. I really fuckin' 'ated them.'

'In our school there was this one girl called Caroline who
said she 'ad the calling. She used to go in on Saturdays for
lessons to become a novice. She's banged up with a junkie
in a caravan now. I think she was a bit like you coz it was
'er mum that wanted her to be a nun, not God.'

'Was she Irish?'

'No.'

'I'm surprised.'

'Why? Are you Irish?'

'No, but I notice a lot of the nuns are Irish. I thought
it might be hereditary.' He looked at me to tell me he was
only kidding.

'Maybe it's because there's loads of Irish in and around
Liverpool so you notice it more,' I said, ignoring his look
coz I was interested in this Irish angle.

'Maybe. They're much holier than the English, don't yer
think?' he said, carrying it on a bit further.

'They go from one extreme to the other though, don't
they? I mean they either 'ave tons of kids or don't 'ave
any at all and lock 'emselves up in a nunnery. I think
they're mad.'

'There's loads of Irish priests. I think loads of 'em didn't
really wanna be priests else they wouldn't 'ave been trying
to screw *us* all the time, would they? They think it's like
being a doctor or a lawyer except if they can't be one

120

o' them, then they blag God into thinkin' they can be a priest. Then all they have to do is 'ope the 'ousekeeper's broad-minded.'

'I used to think our nuns were a bit dodgy, yer know. I used to get to school early so I could 'ave a fag and that, and there were priests coming out of all the exits. I reckon they were bang at it.'

'Prob'ly were.'

He went quiet. He genuflected at the exit to the cathedral and then looked out to Liverpool. He looked like they'd buggered the living daylights out of him.

He wanted to show me the Cavern where the Beatles started out. We fell out of a back alley, 'a short cut', he said, and were just cutting across a main road when we heard men chanting. Like a football crowd. I carried on walking. He stopped.

'Come on,' I said. 'It's only fans.'

'No, it's not. It's the National Front.'

'Is it 'ell. It's Saturday. They're on the way to the match.'

'I'm tellin' yer. It's the National Front.'

The chanting got louder. The 'fans' closer. There wasn't much red and white, it was true. They were rounding a corner ahead, first ten, then twenty. Then too many. I looked around. I was the only black. There weren't that many cars or people. I just walked on reckoning on their bark being worse. Kevin pulled me back. He was terrified.

'If we walk quickly they'll spot yer and run after us. If we go slow they'll catch up. You'll 'ave to hide.'

He was more scared than I was. I let him do what he

had to do which was to hide me in a closed-down shop doorway whilst they marched and jeered their way past.

'WE DON'T NEED NO NIGGERS, WE DON'T NEED NO NIGGERS. TRA LA LA LA,' clap, clap, 'TRA LA LA LA.'

I enjoyed that. Being looked after. When I got up from crouching down, he had a funny look in his eye. Like he was re-drawing me on a new piece of paper. I didn't like that. I didn't know who I was for a minute.

We went to a student café which was full of wood and fruit and apple juice and muesli. It was like being on holiday. Kevin was calmer. He began to tell me all about vegetarians. He agreed with them but after our nut biscuits and decaffeinated coffee we went and got a giant hot dog outside Lime Street Station. Then we went to a shopping centre and Kevin bought a book about philosophy and a new needle for his record player. I didn't buy a thing. I didn't want anything.

We went to a pub which had a sports car hanging from the roof and I nearly got battered by a black woman because I couldn't stop staring at her Afro. It was massive. She asked me what I was 'stirring at' and if I wanted to go outside and talk about it. I 'stirred' into my drink after that.

When we arrived back at the nurses' home, we went to his room to listen to music. He played some Lou Reed. 'It's Such a Perfect Day'. We slept, top 'n' tail, in his bed. I slept like a baby.

In the morning he put his face next to mine when he brought me a cup of coffee. I coughed in it and asked him for a fag. I told him I didn't fancy him. He told me he wanted to screw every nurse in the hospital. He was still a virgin.

He never bothered me in the week when I was with Sylvie

and at weekends we drifted into a drinking relationship. I told him bits of my life story and he seemed pleased to meet someone just as fucked up as himself.

Sylvie was not fucked up. She came from a warm loving family and had a warm loving relationship with Chipper. She was devoted to Chipper who she saw once in the week and again at weekends. He *looked* like a wet weekend. He had a droopy moustache which was too old for him (he was only twenty) and a droopy expression to make it fit better. He rode a motor bike and it was this that Sylvie was in love with. When she showed me photographs of him, she always pointed out the bikes in the background. Chipper in the foreground was the connective tissue. When she talked about their weekends together she said words like 'banking' and 'wheelies', 'raz' and 'tracking', 'sparks' and 'skidding'. I was more jealous of the bike than I was of Chipper.

There were twelve weeks of school and twelve weekends. Each week we spent the odd day on the ward, practising all we learned. What went on in the nurses' school with its plastic dolls clad in royal-blue tracksuits bore little resemblance to the activities going on in live wards, full of the general public often half dead. Everything in school was perfect. The 'procedures' went like clockwork. The oranges, injected with tap water, didn't move about and squirm. The sheets were easy to change even with a doll in the way. How much does a doll weigh? When the doll fell on the floor after dragging it out of the bed, it didn't need a doctor or a lawyer. Plastic dolls don't get pressure sores either. They went on and on about pressure sores in school, or bedsores as they called them in the olden days. I thought it would take weeks and weeks of lying in bed before the pressure got so bad it made a hole in your bum. Not so. Holes that were as big and black as black puddings, I saw. After just a few days. Until I saw such holes I thought they were getting me at it, going round the ward rubbing men's bottoms. I slept like a revolving door for weeks.

Once the true nursing began, it was the weekends that were waved goodbye to, not me. And the nursies took on their martyr pose. The angel pose with their polygonic haloes. The harder they worked, the more they glowed with self-worth, pride. They were proud to be enslaved. They awarded themselves medals, a bottle of perfume, a new LP, a lie in.

After a day on the ward, the workers with stained dresses swung through the kitchen door and let it slam loudly. They were home. They were shifted. And all those who go by must know. Shifted. A loud sigh of relief. Two cheeks full of blow-out, a fringe of blond hair rising from the wind of the mouth. The upper lip sweated and shiny. The arms at last at rest across the kitchen table. A rest of just a minute. Before reaching for a kettle and getting on with the work of relaxing. The hat pulled off. The pins slung across the table. The hair set to rest hanging limp in remembrance of its daytime manipulation. The body slouched in a chair, the back acute to the horizontal. Then to pick up the *Nursing Times*, skip the pages on pressure sores and look at all the pictures of babies with no skin and then say 'Aaaah!'. Fag packets artistically scattered across the kitchen table, ash in its ashtray, pocket watch, plastic bottle tops, scraps of paper with notes scrawled on, sweets, boiled and sticky, covered in fluff, scissors, chains with keys on, tiny address books, lipsalves, biros, coins, mini Melolin pads, hotel butter packs, teaspoons, tissues, buttons, hair slides, elastic bands, half-smoked fags, sweat band. All of these things from the pocket of a nurse.

Then the next shift arrived to do the same. Twenty-four-hour table duty. Always someone on kitchen-table duty, at eight, five and eight. Bang bang. In out. Machine on.

I arrived on the ward at 7.45 a.m. for my first full day of real nursing. Sister Bleek wasn't grinning.

'Nurse, you're late.'

'I thought . . . seven-forty-five?' I was showing her my watch like she didn't have one staring me in the face.

'I like to let the night staff go at seven-forty-five. Now they'll have to wait till eight. I'd like you here for seven-thirty on an early and eleven-thirty on a late. Everyone knows I work that way.'

Delivered with derision. Was she going to make me run around the hospital a hundred times dragging a mental patient on de-housed perambulator wheels? I looked at the faces of my team of nurses. We weren't going to have half as much fun as that. All gathered round Beaky ready for the off.

'Right. Hodges. Bed 1. Steady night. Chron bron. Fifty-eight. Urine infection. Co-trimoxazole tds. Paracetamol prn. Suspected ca lung. Temp steady. Four-hour bp and tpr and plenty of fluids. Stay in bed.

'Howard. Sixty-eight. Bed 2. Ca lung. Lots of tlc. Not for resusc. Steady night. Stay in bed. Turn two-hourly.

'Brown. Thirty-two. New admission. Bed 3. In for stabilisation. Twenty-eight lines per day. Insulin as per card. Came in hyper. What's hyper, Nurse? You. Nurse O' Leary. Hyper. How do you know if someone's hyperglycaemic?'

I jumped out of the steady pose I'd adopted which made me look alert. I was catching up on brain sleep lost the night before on the worry rack.

'Thirst? Lots of thirst?'

'And?'

'Going to the toilet a lot?'

'Getting closer. What else?'

'I don't know.'

'Well, would you test urine?'

'Yep. Test the urine.'

'What for?'

'Ketones.'

'Well, yes, Nurse, if things have gone too far, but what about before ketones? Sugar, Nurse. Sugar in the urine. Anyway, he can get up now. Next, Smithers. Bed 4. Sixty-five . . .'

And so it went on for another twenty-six patients. I'd forgotten what was wrong with everybody from Bed 4 to Bed 23. After the report was over the nurses exploded like a bomb, walking this way and that, fast and busy. I just stood there.

'You go with June. She'll show you what to do.'

I followed June who didn't have any stripes on her hat.

'Right, bed baths. Go and get the bath trolley and make sure you put plenty of inco pads on it.'

June was off to the kitchen to finish her tea.

I set off with deliberate stride to the bathrooms. The sister and the staff nurse shot off to the office to talk about what had really gone on the night before.

I waited like a fool for June to tell me who was going to get the bed-bath treatment first. I was alone on the ward.

Except for the patients. I stood in the middle of them all, holding on to the bath trolley, the way I did as a child holding on to the supermarket trolley, only this time the beans were human. They moved.

A man from behind called me. I went over to him. He was seventy if a day. He couldn't talk properly, his voice hoarse, his breath short. He took his hand from inside the sheets and pointed downwards. Under his bed was a bottle, a grey papier-mâché bottle. I picked it up and offered it to him. It was empty. He pointed towards his thighs, gesturing that I should help him. I pulled back the bedclothes and then thought better of it, seeing all the other men looking. I pulled the curtains round him and carried on. He wanted me to put his willy in the bottle. I didn't want to. I really didn't want to. It was eight o'clock in the bloody morning.

I looked at his face, his eyes dull with despair. His mouth an upside-down banana. His manner was of impatience, almost anger. His arm movements were rigid and desperate. He was either dying for a piss or dying to cover himself up or both. His pyjamas fitted badly. Hospital pyjamas with gaping holes where buttons once were. His chest a living tablecloth stained with tea. It was definitely tea because the leaves still clung to his hairs like nits. I nudged his willy into the right position with the end of the bottle and rested it between his thighs. I pulled the bedclothes back over him and squeezed his shoulder. He gave me a thin tremor of appreciation. Then I left.

When I came out, June was in the middle of a bed bath. Hodges had shit the bed.

I didn't like seeing men with their pants down. Shit. Grown men. Grown-up. Ex-teachers and managers of shops. White sagging flesh, wrinkled, blue-veined man. Face hanging over the side of the bed. Blood rushing to the gills. Breath hard and sorry. Two bitches wiping his bollocks. It comes to this. It comes to this. June was gentle with her cloth but viciously efficient.

'All right, Mr Hodges. Does that feel better? We'll make yer a cup o' tea in a minute,' and stuff like that. Stuff to fill in the gap between the whop of the inco pad, the paddle of the sponge in the water. Stuff to make him fit into his bed. He didn't fit into his bed any more than we fitted into our uniforms, us new nurses.

There were pictures of his grandchildren. But no pictures of men from the office, workmates. No pictures of his schoolmates. No memory of all that life. As though all that life was really worthless. His wife was dead. His wife was alive. What did it matter? School, work, the shops, the neighbours. They are nothing to a man who was a company director, lying with his arse to the world, letting a girl like me wipe shit out of his rectum, clean out his mouth with pink sponges, tie him in his bed with white strict sheets, done and dusted and on to the next. Jesus.

Damp November winter and the ward filled up with chronbrons thick and fast. Most of 'em smoked, lived in damp houses and ate chips and bacon and stuff like that. In school, they told us this was why they got chronbron. By December, the chronbrons had taken over.

The auxiliary, June, said they only came in for Christmas, half of 'em. They could go to the day ward and smoke their heads off. In January they'd be back home again. Often relatives refused to take them home for Christmas. Chronic bronchitis. I always thought it was just a bad cough. OK.

A chronically bad cough. Take some cough mixture and get to bed. Some of the men on this ward looked like they were dying of it. And then some did. My first death wasn't a chronbron. He was a CVA. A CVA is someone who's had a stroke, or a cerebral vascular accident. Like a road accident in the motorways of the brain, I thought. Charles the CVA.

It was Charles that made Sister Bleek like me. He couldn't move. He could have moved one side of his body if he could have been bothered but he wasn't bothered. He was hacked off and I couldn't blame him. Before being involved in a brain accident, he was a marketing manager for a big car factory. He was fat. Used to smoke. Had dead posh green pyjamas and plenty of them. They all looked new. Ironed in shirt folds good enough for John Lewis's. His face was red and his hair white and curly. His chubby stumped legs were white and cold and sort of childish-looking. Nurses held beakers to his mouth. Sat by his bed and stuffed food in his mouth. Mashed the food up toddler-style and then played with it for something to do. Between mouthfuls. Looked at patients on the other side of the ward and shouted instructions out to them while Charles was trying to eat his dinner. Charles stopped trying in the end and went on a drip.

He deteriorated very quickly. I changed his drips for him. Frusemide and saline. He couldn't speak. The stroke damaged the left side of his brain. The side that does all the talking. I doubt he would have done much yapping, whatever side it was on. The damage.

He was duffed up to death, pillows everywhere. Keep the airway open. Keep pressure from the paralysed limbs. Turn him. Turn him. Turn him. His baby bottom, round and baby pink, was not like his jaw, wide and manly. I was changing his drip once when the relatives arrived. Four of them. The rule was two to a bed but nobody took a blind bit of notice of that. They sat round his bed and talked. To each other. He just lay there. Listening. They couldn't understand that just because he wasn't yapping didn't mean he was a goner. I caught his expression. He was telling me to send them away. How did I know that? Because I asked him.

When they'd gone, I sat by his bed and did the two squeezes for yes, one for no routine. I liked holding his hand. I tried to ask questions that needed a *no* answer so that he didn't have to do much squeezing, but sometimes it had to be yes answers and sometimes I just didn't know what the answers would be.

'Do you like your relatives coming to see you?'
One squeeze.
'Do you wish you were dead?'
One squeeze.
'Do you want something to drink?'
One squeeze.
'How many children have you got?'
One squeeze.

I knew he had three kids so I guessed we weren't communicating that well. Mind you, only two of them had been to see him.

'Would you like me to make you more comfortable?'
Two squeezes. Bingo.

That took ages – making him more comfortable – and when I got the reassuring two squeezes that I'd done it, I thought about trying to be a proper nurse.

The drip came down the next day and he asked for

breakfast. I fed him. I held his hand afterwards and then he died on me.

Sister Bleek and I laid him out. I hadn't told anybody up until then about my little chats with Charles. She knew though.

'Look, Nurse, it's not as easy as you think it might be.'

'What d'yer mean?'

She was really gentle with him. She took all his pillows away and laid him flat like he was still alive. Gentle. She fingered his eyes so's to keep them from rolling about in front of us. She stuffed cotton wool up his back passage. And up his nose. It was running a bit. I stood watching.

'Straighten his legs, Nurse.'

I felt close to her, just her and me and Charles. Charles all clean and shrouded up ready for the Lord. Sister all calm, almost like the heat was off. The engine had stopped running. There was a tranquillity within our curtains, a sort of reverence to the monstrous god that had been delivered another human. A silence. Charles, dead, asked for more than he did alive. He wanted more dignity. More care to be taken with his belongings, his nails, his feet. This was difficult to do because Sister Bleek wanted me to tie his feet together and I thought it was a bit rotten on Charles to tie him up like a chicken when what he really wanted was to be let free. In his shroud, he looked like he was playing the part of an angel in a school nativity play, waiting for his wings. I wanted my own personal shroud for when I died. Not a white one from the hospital.

'Yer see, whilst you've been mollycoddling him and squeezing his fingers for the past forty-eight hours, we've

131

been doing your work. I know it's hard but you must realise there's too much to do to have personal favourites.'

'He's not my favourite. I just thought he wanted someone to talk to. His relatives just sat around talking past him, to each other. I felt sorry for him.'

'Well, that's commendable but not very practical, I'm afraid.'

She threw me a grin that was big enough to make me forget about poor dead Charles. Sister Bleek liked me.

Chapter 15

Alone, in my bed, I thought of the men. In jamas. Smelly toilets. Willies. On the streets men do up their trousers, their flies. Put it away. Neat and tidy. In the ward I saw open holes in jamas. Dark holes that went to the organ. Flaccid, brown-stained, bent and wrinkled with worry and wear. No barrier. No underpants. Just skin, willy and hair. Dark hairs and smells to spill out into my young unworked fingers. Slit of filthy dark secret. Smells of sweated scents of toilet robbing the vanity, oozing truth out of its secret space and in my face to do with as directed. Soap it, hold it, move it, watch it, help it. See it opened out. Parted slit, jamas to the knees, bottom dimpled and forgotten by the run and the sun, the pounce, the trouser smart. Men with hair and skin spare enough to stretch back to a teenage romp.

And when I wasn't thinking of men, alone in my bed . . . I was with one. A man set to spill out his all and have my fingers caress his balls, his wherewithal. Such men I found down the pub. As I became more familiar, less foreign and more relaxed, such men on missions tried to pick me up. Men on missions of a one-night screw, of a 'How do you do? How about you?' Pickin' their way over me, us, the doctors' leftovers. Like gulls, feeding on us, getting their fill.

It took a few goes before this pattern emerged. Till I spotted a couple of gulls necking at the bar. Necking girls with full-on face, writhing on the stools. And both of those men had had the pleasure of my bed. Then I saw them resting their elbows on the bar, surveying the galleon of the room, the swaying of the rig, the backsides of the crew. Eyeing up the supply of nurses skint, battle-weary, with a glint in their eye. Predators from the outside world, all in the pub for a stab at a nurse.

And with each new intake of nurses, the landlord, captain of the ship, was always assured of fresh stock. Fresh stock to fill his pub on an ongoing basis, from the casual half-lager drinkers, to the nurses who made it their off-duty duty to be out and about for a flirt or a fuck or just a way out of the nurses' home.

The local boys and some not so local followed their instincts. Their instincts went like this:

'Ere, love! Can I get yer a drink? . . . Psssst . . . D'yer wanna drink?'

'Pernod and black, please, ta!'

'Double?'

'If yer want.'

'Yer look dead smart dancin' an' that. Bet yer look fit in yer uniform, eh?'

'You should know.'

'Know what?'

'If I look fit in me uniform.'

'Should I?'

'Does a large pink teddy bear ring any bells?'

'Eh?'

'Marmite on toast. Three o'clock in the morning?'

'Oh I'm with yer. I spewed up on yer teddy, didn't I? Jesus. Fancy forgettin' that. How is he? God, it was grim that night, wasn't it? Your fault, mind. Southern Comfort. Eh! Look at yer! Yer lookin' great! Lost a bit o' the old flab there, 'aven't yer?'

'No.'

'D'yer wanna drink?'

'Yer just asked me that. Pernod and black, please. Double.'

'Look! Yer mate's wavin' at yer. Shall I get her one? What? Vodka and orange? Right. On its way.'

'If I remember right, you work on the rigs, don't yer? Yer must be loaded.'

'Yeah, that's right. Yer remembered. Jesus! Look at yer knockin' the bevvy back. I'm not that loaded.'

'It's me day off tomorrow.'

'Oh that's all right then. I'll get yer another . . . Oh I see . . . off for another dance now, are we? I'll 'ang on 'ere for yer . . . all right?'

There was usually a couple of hours of that, the boys watching the girls dancing, the girls watching the boys watching and the boys sending the landlord sailing round the Mediterranean, six weeks a year, every year. By the time last orders were up, the boys had a nurse under one arm, some cans of beer under the other, and, pissed as farts, dragged their trophies back to the nurses' home. And then came the game.

One night I managed a particularly good-looking drummer. Italian. Very nice. I needed someone. Just for the night like. We did the routine, drinking, dancing, watching.

With the nurses off the landing, some with one-nighters, others with fiancés, we left the pub to make our way back to the nurses' home. From the pub doorway, we could see the home, massive and black behind the streetlights. Walled in, silent, grim. Made us feel small. We had to walk in walking tall.

The boys went round the back. We fronted ourselves to the warden. Laughing. Pissed. She was an eighteenth-century model, buttoned up to the neck, tight-lipped in the grip of responsibility for our well-being.

She unlocked the door to let us in, no trace of a grin, let alone a good-night, and in the inspecting light of the porch, we caught her glassy stare and returned it with our spiteful glares. She rattled keys to tell us she'd got the gist. She flicked her wrist as a jailer on the lock, locking us into her mighty castle of the grim. Our lips were loose and loud, our bodies rolled in laughter.

We ignored her position, that of being in charge of our lives, begging for our spiteful glares behind the door. True to form, she got what she asked for. Then we danced down the corridors towards our block. One of us on the lookout ... Keep a look. Keep a look.

'She's comin'.'

We shouted out the windows to tell the lads to hang on. They were lying down in the grasses like soldiers. There were spotlights out there and security men that stalked.

'Stay,' we say, shouting, whispering. 'Stay.'

We wait behind our doors. Our sex and saliva pumping. Our fingers drumming the backs of our doors. Waiting. I'm tidying my room in readiness for my Italian. Then the lookout goes to check. Back down to the end of the landing.

'All's clear.'

She puts her thumb up to tell us. Then down the back stairs to the fire escape.

I lean out the window and say, 'It's clear.'

The lads lift up the wire fence and shimmy underneath, walking on their forearms. After they are under, they do a ten-yard dash to the fire-escape door, one after the other, the lookout looking out and about. And then up the stairs in five-step leaps. Up to our landing. All the time they are giggling like schoolkids, sucking in air to drown out the laughing. They are drunk and wild for wenches. Once they're on the landing, we show the boys to our respective rooms. Like whores.

My Italian fell in like a Colditz hero. We got straight down to it. More drink. Music. Fighting. Laughing. Throwing each other about the room and then a knock at the door. It's the warden.

'Nurse O'Leary, do you have a visitor in there?'

'Nope.'

'Can I come in to take a look?'

'Nope.'

I can hear her keys rattling but my keys are in the lock on the inside so she won't be able to open my door. But she's trying.

'Well, the noise you're making tells me there is someone in there.'

'That's my radio.'

I stuffed two pillows over the head of my Italian to smother him.

'Well, can you keep the radio down, please. You'll wake up the block.'

'Certainly.'

'Security are on the fences all night and all morning, so if you're lying . . .'

The next morning I was on a late. On the ward. On the ward where I injected insulin. Regulated and monitored intravenous solutions. Gave oxygen. Set up trolleys for lumbar punctures. Did cardiac massage. Watched epilepics go into *grand mals*. Undressed gangrenous toes. Fed Ryle's tubes up people's noses and down to their stomachs. Put faeces on the end of a spatula and then put it in a plastic carton. Then labelled it.

Or said to Mr Bride, 'Spit in here, Mr Bride, if yer don't mind. That's right, bring it up. A really good cough. Then spit . . . in this little cup.'

I gave Largactil to the mad. I laid out the dead. I watched men cry and watched them die. But I couldn't have one in my room.

Fulfilling the role of Colditz hero, my Italian walked out on a wet Wednesday morning, wearing a white coat with a stethoscope sticking out of his pocket. Walking past the warden, wide-eyed and smiling, with a 'Good morning' and a baby bow of the head, he was out in the grounds to meet me. The white coat and the tie and the 'scope went under my cape and back to the landing to be used again by some other bloke. The warden couldn't, no, wouldn't, say a dickie bird to a doctor. The doctors were staff. Allowed on the premises. Allowed to screw the nurses. What could she say? They had a free run. Like headless chickens they ran true to form in a pecking-order of cocks. Running amok in our home.

138

I had to be really drunk to be bothered with all that palaver, to screw a bloke who looked better than passable and was definitely pissed.

Kevin, being staff, had the same freedom as the doctors. But not the invitations. So near but yet so far. But then he did have some luck and when I saw him, he could hardly contain himself. He told me before we got to Mr George. Before we put our masks on.

He was catheterising Mr George and I was his assistant. The male nurse on our ward was off sick so they asked Kevin to come over. It was better for a male patient if a man did it, but sometimes it couldn't be helped and it had to be a female. I preferred doing the men. I hated doing the women. It made my skin crawl.

The catheter tube itself is the same colour as a jiffy bag. First Kevin has to clean the area of the penis – inside the foreskin. I have to stand by the trolley passing him things. We pretend we're in an operating theatre. He plays along with me.

'Saline, please . . . Syringe, please.'

I pass as directed, smirking under my mask.

The poor patient lying there, displaying his wherewithal. Actually I don't think he needs a catheter. If they gave him a chance to relax, settle down, ran taps of water by him for a couple of hours, he'd probably get along fine.

But they say, 'No.'

His feet were bloated up with water and his rag-doll legs didn't waist-in at the ankles. The pressure of the water on his heart was dangerous. His skin dimpled to moon-surface craters when I pressed my fingertips in.

'Catheter, please, Nurse.'

139

Kevin rolls back the foreskin and puts the catheter tube in the tip of the penis. The catheter's about as thick in diameter, maybe a diddy bit smaller than . . . say . . . phone cable. Not the curly bit on the handle. The bit that goes in the wall. Kevin feeds it slowly down the penis.

'Might feel a little bit uncomfortable, Mr George.'

Not might. Bloody well does.

Mr George is being brave. He has to be. I'm there. The men don't like to squirm in front of the women. Once he's finished feeding the tube in, Kevin wants to squirt water down it and asks for the syringe. At this point, when Mr George sees the size of the carriage on the syringe, he does much squirming.

Kevin starts shouting. Nurses do that. They think all patients are deaf.

'It's all right, Mr George. We're just going to inject some water into your catheter. Test it out. It'll be all right.'

Mr George relaxes. His willy looks really uncomfortable with the tube stuck out of the end. It's easy to do the men though. Take aim and fire. Bang on. Every time. Women's wee-holes are all over the place. Rooting around for it is no fun, and sticking a tube down it even less of a giggle. And don't be fooled by the lignocaine, the local, as they call it. General is what is required.

When we were getting the trolley ready for Mr George, Kevin told me he had a date that night with a nurse called Bridget, an Irish nurse. She was small and very pretty. Bit over the top with the make-up, I thought, but a lot of the nurses went in for that sort of thing. She was well doctored, I knew. Liam the houseman told me all about her. Kevin was in good hands.

The underground sex shop at the hospital loosened

tension, wove intrigue and provided both nurses interested and doctors very interested with a challenge off duty. Over at the pub, the doctors kept a list of unfucked nurses. When they had parties, called Doctors' Res parties, they invited all the good-fuck and unfucked nurses and shared them out amongst each other. Then they rewrote the list accordingly.

They weren't interested in me though they liked me well enough. The boys on the dole in the parks of my adolescence didn't want to fuck me so I figured those doctors with the pick of hundreds of white women with their tongues hanging out weren't going to be any different. There was no way I was gonna make a fool of myself trying.

For the doctors, sex was something they could get to grips with. Twenty-four hours a day it was possible, available. Like them. Bleepers bleeped all through their nights, their lives. Young men and women like the walking dead themselves, some of them. They needed sex. The patients were very liquid. They flowed in and out and disappeared overnight.

A lot of them dying. Cheyne-Stoking for days. Cheyne-Stokes respirations that wax and wane. Deep noisy gasps that sound like life itself is hanging on to the phlegm of the lung, like loosening glue or melting cheese off a pizza. Then quiet breaths with no noise. Nearly all over. Nearly dead. And each time the quiet breaths came, I hoped they were dead. But then they started up again, like the rattling chains of the slaves after rest. Standing up, arranging the shackles around their feet to make themselves a little more comfortable, and then on again, on the journey to hell or wherever. I wanted to drag them up the bed and smack the living daylights out of them when they did that. But they were too dead to do that to.

Sometimes patients came in and out and I never saw them. Their notes still in the files. If they came in on my day off and died, all I had left was the washing of the bed and the notes. People died all over the place. Young women died of breast cancer; their kids stood at the end of the bed crying. Old women died of life, their sons, like my dad, held their hands, and beat their chests in guilt, for opportunities lost. And when it's all over the black plastic bag is filled with the nighty, the toilet bag, the photo, the jewellery, the magazines. And an old man leaves his wife and his life and goes down the stairs clutching the bin bag to his chest. Then he walks the grounds of the hospital, aimless at first until he decides on a strategy, an exit out of the place. And then he stands at the bus stop waiting. In winter.

Sex was solid, available and alive. A decent distraction.

I was pleased for Kevin. Bridget would teach him a thing or two. Give him a seeing-to. He was so nervous and excited about his date he forgot to close the spigot on the catheter bag and poor Mr George pissed himself all over the floor. He thought he was cured. Said he wanted to go home.

I never saw Kevin for two days after. Or Bridget. Nobody did. He emerged in love. Sun came up on a man sort of thing. It was Bridget this, Bridget that. Bridget said this. Said that. Used to do this. That. An unfortunate development. Because Bridget loved everybody.

I avoided Kevin throughout this affair. He did his work on autopilot. He lived for his time off. A lot of his time off was spent in his room hoping Bridget would visit him. She banned him from her quarters. She said she'd see him when she got the chance. Kevin was pathologically obsessed and he called it love.

My next ward was women's surgical. Sister Casey's ward. She was a friend of Sister Bleek. She was blonde, pretty, petite and had a high-fuck score over in the Doctors' Res. Liam told me all this. But no doctor wanted anything else from her. She was looking to get out of nursing quarters and to move into a three-bedroomed detached in Knowsley. Beaky had me in her office before she handed me over to her.

'Nurse, when you first came on the ward, I thought you had too much lip. Well, I still think that but you've a good positive attitude to nursing, which I like. A lot of nurses do their work blindfold. I notice you notice. You take people's temperatures, which is useful . . . and pulses. I've noticed some of them nurses taking pulses and they haven't even wound up their watches. When I read your charts, I know the observations have been done. That's good. What is not good . . . is your relationship with Liam Cotswold.'

'But I don't have a relationship with Liam Cotswold.'

'That's not what the rumours say.'

'No, but it's what I say. I'm telling the truth. Anyway, even if I was goin' with him, it's not against the law, is it?'

She started taking pins out of her hair. Removing the spears of her status in front of me. Not like Mother Superior who always seemed to be sticking more in. Then she took her cap off and let her fierce hairstyle rest in crimps on her shoulders and across her forehead. Her nose looked smaller. She leant forward on her desk holding her costume cap as if to take a bow. She smiled a really dirty smile.

'No, but it's against Sister Casey's law. She fancies the arse off him.'

Then she burst out laughing. I laughed with her – out of nervousness more than anything else. After all, Beaky was Sister Casey's mate. Supposedly. They were known together as the witches of Mitton because they were so strict. They sat and fagged together in the canteen. Even the other sisters were scared of them. And here I was, laughing with Beaky, laughing at Sister Casey with Beaky Sister Bleek.

But she wasn't just having a goodbye giggle. She had a message to deliver.

'Watch it. She's dead punctual. She likes procedures done by the book. And watch her staff nurse. Casey's right hand. Staff doesn't like coloureds. She's National Front.'

I never associated the National Front with women, with nurses. They were skinheads to me. Bovver boys and yobbos. Yobbos like Gary.

Chapter 16

Mrs Duncan came in. Car accident. She came up from ICU, intensive care, because there was sod all else they could do for her down there. She was middle-forties and mangled to pieces – no amputated limbs or anything. Worse. She was paralysed from the neck down. Completely and permanently. She had internal bleeding, lots of it, and she was a projectile faecal vomiter. That meant she vomited fountains of shit all over the walls – alone. She had a collar round her neck so she couldn't move her head. Her neck was completely broken. She cried silently, all day and all night, because she was in agony – mental agony. It was torture just looking at her so I didn't go into her room unless I had to.

The day before I started on Casey's ward, her right-hand Staff got engaged to a Dr Lempton, a senior house officer. It was a whirlwind romance during which she accidentally got herself pregnant. He asked her to marry him, him being a Catholic. And then Sister Casey froze her out. I was pleased. Poor Sister Casey was still trying to get Liam Cotswold into bed. That he was only a houseman and still resisted only added to her embarrassment, an embarrassment she couldn't vocalise or admit to. But it was loud enough anyway. She couldn't silence it, not now, not ever. If she gave up wanting him, the embarrassment would be added to her CV. If she carried on trying, then the embarrassment just grew fatter and heavier and weighed on her so much that the confirmation she was past it was ever present and evident even to a stranger like me. But other than Dr Charlie Fox who was absolutely ungettable, Liam was the only decent-looking, reasonably discerning doctor worth going for.

Dr Charlie Fox was seriously attached to an occupational therapist called Julie whose beauty was enough to make the crippled sods she treated give up trying from the outset. Such beautiful people are best left behind the perfume counters in John Lewis's where they belong, not trying to convince sixty-year-old stroke victims that they can do it if they really want to – because one look at her said they couldn't. That's what Staff said.

Because he was so ungettable, because his girlfriend was so beautiful, Dr Fox looked lonely. The nurses didn't flirt with him because how could they compare? His girlfriend was grace on the legs of a stork with a face that looked really out of place in a hospital. Her hair was bunned from silk grooves of auburn perfection. Her teeth were painted white between the perfect lipstick of her dark-brown sultry lips. She surrounded herself with ugly people trying to knit, stuttering through the damaged left hemispheres of their brains.

Dr Fox was satisfied. There was no need to add to his life. No need to make him feel any more wanted than he already was. If he'd played the game a bit more, down at the pub, with the scorecards, no doubt he would have found friends among the doctors. But he wouldn't do that. On those nights, he was with her.

Sister Casey had bedded most of the senior housemen and registrars, in the early years of her mission. Snakes and ladders. She got up to square eighty-nine once and then slid all the way back down. Liam could give her a leg up. Get her back into the right society, have her taken to the right parties. She didn't just want to get into his bed, but also his wallet and his bathroom and his motor car that could take her into a life outside the hospital. That's where the real opportunities were.

She wagged her arse down the ward whenever he showed up. Like a small dog, a poodle with a coiffured tail, paws at the ready, on the first rung of her ladder, sitting at the bottom, bow in her hair, she whined at him. She painted her lips with a slim black paintbrush and practised archer accuracy. Her perfume made the sluice room smell like a flower shop.

Staff and her engagement ring were shunned and ignored by Sister Casey. Staff romped past all the snakes and was up all the ladders in a series of double-sixes. Now she was unwanted by Sister, the Sister she'd spent the best part of two years covering up for, demeaning herself for, arranging liaisons for. Now she was getting married she could flirt openly. Everyone knew it was just flirting then, teasing not wanting. Not wanting because she had a ring to prove she was already wanted. Taken. She flirted predominantly with men in white coats. Even the dieticians. She offered them cups of tea and asked them about her fiancé Doug Lempton. Did they know him? Wasn't he marvellous and weren't the house prices in Knowsley just staggering even for a medium-sized four-bedroomed detached? Sister Casey made her do catheterisations, female catheterisations. She put her in charge of emptying all the bags of urine every four hours because the likes of me couldn't be trusted, she said. Catheter bags stink of warm piss in a Wellington boot on a summer's day.

Heather the auxiliary was always off sick with a bad back, the best sick note a nurse can angle for. I was the next most senior allocated to that ward. There was a first-year pupil who was sweet and eager to learn but didn't have a clue. Consequently, Staff could only gossip with me if there weren't any doctors around to slobber at.

She told me she didn't like black people but I was OK. And anyway I wasn't that black. It was the *really* black ones that caused all the trouble. I was relieved. I got the feeling she quite liked me. She made me cups of tea and when it was time for breaks often she organised the ward so that she could go on break with me rather than with the auxiliary or the pupil.

It was on a break that she told me Sister Casey couldn't have kids because she'd had a hysterectomy. Sister Casey would never marry a doctor. She was engaged to one once but she found out he was having an affair and impulsively she threw the ring back at him. Two weeks later, he got engaged to the woman he was having an affair with. Sister Casey was devastated. He was a consultant obstetrician. Him and his new wife had twins. Sister Casey was bitter. Double bitter, I guess. I wondered whether it was him that gave her the hysterectomy but I didn't ask.

Staff always ate doughnuts on her break. With so much practice you'd think she'd've had it sussed but more often than not there'd be jam all over her uniform lapels. Everyone thought it was blood till they got up close. She shouldn't have eaten doughnuts because she was fat. She didn't care though because she was engaged and eating for two.

She asked me what I thought of Sister Casey.

'I think she's all right. I've not really had that much to do with her.'

'Do you think she's pretty?'

'Yep, I suppose so. For her age. How old is she?'

'She's gettin' on if she wants to get married. Mind, who's gonna marry a thirty-odd-year-old woman who can't have kids? Not a doctor. Not when he can have the pick of any nurse he likes. I do feel sorry for her . . . I mean, there's no reason to take it out on me though, is there?'

I didn't answer. I supped my tea and checked my watch for support. Then I checked the clock in the canteen against my watch for even more support. I didn't know what to say. Whatever I said it could or would be used against me.

'She could get married and adopt, I suppose. But it's not the same, is it, not having your own kids? I mean kids from homes – bound to be something wrong with them. Could turn out to be really weird. And anyway all the baby ones go really quickly, don't they? There's only the blacks and the handicapped left and who wants them?'

Quite.

When we got back on the ward Sister Casey went for her break. Mrs Duncan was vomiting. The beds had to be changed and the walls washed down. More air freshener to spray and more fluids to administer. There was no point holding the woman's hand because she couldn't feel a thing. I had to stand over her face and smile and talk to her. It was like looking down a long tunnel with someone stood at the other end, someone I could hardly see even though our heads were inches apart. Whenever I talked to her, even just to tell her the time, tears welled up in her eyes and fell over her temples and round the tops of her ears and I scratched the back of her ear for her, drying the running water with the tips of my fingers.

I was pushing the linen trolley back to the bathroom when I heard Staff shouting.

'Call Crash. Call Crash.'

I looked round the ward. All the patients seemed fine. No one was arresting. No blue faces. The only other patient was Mrs Duncan. Surely she didn't want the Crash team for Mrs Duncan? I ran back down the ward into Mrs Duncan's room and sure enough – she looked like the Ribena man.

'Call Crash,' Staff was screaming at me. The bed-clothes were pulled back and she was thumping the woman's chest.

I had to call Crash. I had to do what I was told. I didn't run. When I phoned, I was quiet and subdued, not in a blind panic how nurses usually are. There was no adrenalin pumping – in anticipation of a res-urrection. When the Crash team flew up the ward, I calmly shouted them back with a 'She's in here' – more like I was showing somebody to their table in a restaurant.

Dr Fox was there. When he saw my face he could see something was up. I left him to it. I didn't stand in the background and watch the firework display of rapid drug input and then climb on my tiptoes to see the fibrillators kick in like a horse. I didn't watch. I sat in the office and wondered what life was really all about. Selfishly and preposterously I wondered what my life was all about. They didn't save her.

Dr Fox came into the office and looked straight at me. I just turned away in disgust.

'Hey, I had to come.'

He was right. He did have to. I realised then I was being a bit cruel. Blaming it on him.

'Yeah, I know,' I said, accepting his apology.

He smiled at me. There was a trace of a smile on my face as I left the office to go up the ward and find Staff. I heard him whistling.

'Why did you try?' I said to her.

She was putting a shroud on the bath trolley and checking there were enough cloths and pads.

'She was only forty-four. We always resuscitate the young ones. Finish doing this, Nurse. I'm going to write my report. I'll make Dr Fox a cup of tea.'

She'd caused a bit of a stir. She had something to write about. She'd seen a few more white coats than she would have done if she hadn't called Crash. She tried her best, she said to Sister Casey when she came back from her break. Sister Casey looked like she wanted to kill. It was embarrassing for her, having all those doctors trying to save the life of a woman that was dead anyway.

Mrs Duncan waited for the porters to take her to the mortuary. I was glad she won.

Chapter 17

I drank cider to help me sleep through the din. Empty bottles lined the walls of my room. I was on the second row in less than two months. I stole road lights from the roadworks outside the hospital and set them flashing in the dark. It felt like I had company. Or I just felt mad.

No one was allowed in. It was my only space and I wanted to control it. All of it. Introspecting. I saw a kaleidoscope of whirring hospitals and nurses, their boyfriends, the house with the front lawn and the wooden gate, the children, the man, drunk and copulating, the life. I didn't see me in any of the sections. Each section had white people in, some with white hats on – some just smiling and stroking each other. There wasn't a *me* at the window in the house, waving to the husband and holding the child. There wasn't a *me*.

Kevin called round and we went to the pub. He was really fidgety. He'd grown spots since I last saw him and he was picking at them, taking them in turns and curling hair behind his ear like a girl. I hadn't seen very much of him and I hoped that Bridget was out of his head.

'How's yer sex life?'

'Oh that's all over.'

'No, Kevin. Yer sex life isn't over. Bridget is. That's different.'

'That's what she said about me. I just don't know with her. Actually, I was gonna tell yer before . . . There's a bit o' trouble with Bridget.'

'Oh God, Kevin! She's not pregnant?'

'No, nothin' like that. But she could be in trouble. I saw this animal Tokyo Joe down her corridor last week. Well, before that, I saw 'em together, dancin' down the pub. He was all over her. And yer know what they're like, that lot. Tokyo Joe's lot, I mean. So when I saw him down her corridor, wanderin' about aimlessly, I reckoned, well, I figured it was best if his sort wasn't hanging round our nurses' home at all – all them women there and that. So I grassed him up to the warden. He's been caught twice before apparently. By security. So the police were called. The warden must've told the police that it was a male nurse that alerted her coz the first thing Bridget said to me, next time I went to see her, was, "You – Male Nurse – go and play with yerself." She told me to stay away from her and her corridor. Quite angry, she was. I'll get her to come round, though. But for now, I'm in the shit. And Jesus, the man's an animal. What the fuck does she wanna be with him for?'

Given the seriousness of these developments, I was surprised to see him looking for a blue twist of paper in his crisp bag, a blue twist of salt. He was disappointed when he found a sachet. That wasn't what he was looking for.

'Sounds to me like you and Bridget are history, and so will *you* be if yer don't watch out.'

'Well, I'm still gonna try!'

153

'Don't be so pathetic, Kevin! After that! 'Ave you got a death wish, or what? I wouldn't wanna clap eyes on the girl ever again. Specially if she's been with him.'

'She's all right. She's really nice when yer get to know her.'

'Tokyo Joe isn't, Kevin. He's a villain. Nutty family! There's about twenty of 'em. Brothers and sisters. Mini-mafia. I'd steer clear if I were you.'

I heard about Tokyo Joe's clan from the nurses in casualty. Without *them* living in the area, the hospital could have saved a few grand on ambulances and beds, they said. Kneecaps and hammers were their speciality and maybe more seriously, nose and ear removal. Luckily Mitton Hospital specialised in plastic surgery which was either handy or historical. No one knew which.

The clan had dogs that they trained to attack policemen by using a policeman's helmet as a target. One poor policeman lost most of his willy after one of their dogs got hold of it. They trained the dogs to do that. Specially. They were evil. They lived in two houses knocked into one and paid for by the council. They weren't council houses either. No one on a council estate would live next door to them. So they were given really nice houses in a meadow away from people. Every now and again one of them got shot during target practice, which, because they lived in a meadow, they did a lot of. They used the casualty department the way other people use a DIY store.

'Oh I don't give a shit about Tokyo Joe,' said Kevin. 'They can't be interested in a squirt like me.'

'No, I suppose you're right.'

'I'm really pissed off though, yer know. Not just coz of Bridget. Well, it's everything really. D'yer know what

I mean? I mean what's it all for? Why do we bother? It's the age-old question, isn't it?' He was swigging his pint too fast and making a mess.

'What age-old question?'

'The meaning of life. Philosophers from time immemorial have asked the same question. What is the meaning of life?'

'And?'

'And there is no meaning to life. Why is a flower a flower? Why do people pray? Because there is no meaning to life. Praying is a human fiction made up to handle the stress of knowing that there is no meaning to life. An invention to . . .'

''Ang on a minute. Who the fuck rattled your cage? I don't want a friggin' lecture, Kevin.'

'Yeah, OK, but listen a min. I've sussed it. Our life boils down to two things and two things only. Sex and money. I've got this really good book. It tells you everything you need to know about the meaning of our life. You'd like it. It goes on about being manipulated by governments. About keeping rich people rich and poor people poor. It says that governments use people to do just that. They don't care about life and meaning and all that. They just want a good time. And really, we're all like that. We just want money and sex. We are part of what makes the government a government. We put them there.'

'Sounds riveting, Kevin.'

I didn't want money or sex. Well, some money would have been all right. I wouldn't have knocked it back. Pools money, tons of money. Bits of money aren't much use. A three per cent pay rise? Me and Kevin drank one of them every time we went to the pub. And we *needed* the pub.

He looked smug and satisfied with himself when he was talking about the book. Because he'd sussed out life and all its meaning, worrying about Tokyo Joe was like worrying about the Lecky bill when the house has just burnt down. That's what he said.

'This book isn't a story. It's not fiction. It's about us. Where we live. *This Is Your Society*, it's called. I'll get it for yer when we get back.'

Sylvie finished with Chipper and got herself a motor bike instead. Wow!

Our backs got really bad after that. Our doctor was great. He gave us what we wanted when we wanted. Sick notes and pills. We nurses were next to nuns in the queue for heaven. That close to God. Give them what they need. I had a windowsill full of Distalgesics and Equagesics. All the other nurses had plant pots.

On our sick days we went biking with no lids on, round Delamere Forest and sometimes down the M62, the police in hot pursuit, but they never caught us. Delamere was outer space. So many trees. I wondered who put them there and why. Why plant so many trees? Why use up all that space just for trees? I liked it.

Inside the woods it wasn't the way I felt inside a building. In the rain, Delamere was one big umbrella. Naked trees. They could feel us inside them, walking about, but they didn't mind. I knew. I could tell. There was a welcome . . . I know that's a song but there was a welcome in those trees. There was nothing we could do to hurt them.

Sylvie got bored easily and wanted to ride around all the time. It was a trials bike and the mud was good. I let her. I stayed and wandered between the tree-trunk legs of the old men and the thighs of the nubile women. I hugged them. Put my face up to them and said 'Hello'. This was all done private like. Sylvie was way off on her bike. I shouted and made myself feel small. I sat and made myself invisible, after finding a tree the same colour as me. I cried and made myself feel stupid.

Back at the ranch we played music together and sometimes Sylvie slept in my bed, top 'n' tail. I loved her. Sometimes she refused to sleep in my bed. Said she wanted to be alone. I didn't want that. Not when I was lonely. I needed someone I really . . . well, it's not love, is it? When it's your mate? It's somat else. But I was lonely for it nevertheless.

Sometimes I pushed her. Sometimes I pushed her hard. I said, 'Please, not tonight. I can't be on my own tonight,' and she changed her mind and got in my bed. At first she was quiet but then I started. I'd say something to make her feel sorry for me so she had no choice but to answer me or risk hurting me. I gave that girl hell. I was a bit worried in case I fancied her. I didn't know. I couldn't imagine kissing her. The idea of it made me squirm. Lesbians were thin on the ground then. I didn't want to be one of them.

After Casey's ward came theatre. I didn't squeam at the blood. It was interesting. Exciting. When the inside of a body came outside, when the bone entered the world through a leg, it was science fiction made real. I loved the reality. I loved seeing bone, sharp and pink white – seared skin. In class they drew bones on the blackboard. In life we saw them drawn out of the body by hands scrubbed and gloved. Great stuff.

The costumes were ridiculous. Slip-on white shoes,

anti-static. Green gowns that tie up the back. Masks. Scientifically proven to be ineffective after forty-five seconds. J-cloth hats to cover the hair. Pyjamas in green or yellow. In theatre, there was no telling who was who. Everyone wore the same clothes, some elegantly, some not so. Them with the gloves on were the ones doing the business.

Eyes were very important in theatre because the rest of the facial expression was obscured by the masks. I saw people shouting at me with their eyes. Trying to get me to do things. They couldn't speak, perhaps because that moment of the operation was crucial, perhaps because the surgeon didn't allow speaking, unless it was in relation to his patient. Perhaps because they didn't want to bother. Some just liked to boss us with their eyes. Wouldn't waste their breath.

Then there was the anaesthetist. He, and it usually was a he, had a joke machine, a Doctor Who contraption that he wheeled about so close to him you'd think *his* life depended on it. I hate to go back to sci-fi but that box of his was like a dinner trolley with arms and legs – pipes and pumps – and a mind of its own. The anaesthetist looked like he was scared of it. It was always there at the top of the bed, next to the head of the patient. When the patient was wheeled in, already out for the count, the mask went on. Then the gas man fiddled about with pipes and gauges, looked at charts and confirmed how much kosh the patient was going to get. Enough to keep them koshed for a whole operation, it was hoped, but not always achieved. Boring job that, anaesthetist. He had to sit by the patient's head all through the operation. We could walk round. We could dance if there wasn't anybody watching.

There were six theatre rooms on one side of the hospital and two on the other. The smaller site did operations on ears, noses and throats. Tonsils and grommets. Very boring. Although they did say that a tonsillectomy was the second most dangerous operation after open-heart surgery. The risk of bleeding. I don't know if that was true. I think they were just getting us at it. Trying to make it sound more exciting.

On the big site all sorts went on, amputations, plastic surgery, varicose veins, heart surgery, Caesarean sections and terminations. They were birthing them in one room and bottling them in another.

In the birthing theatre, the women awake watched as their bellies were slit wide open and from the domes of cascading blood fountains their babies entered the world, carried up into the air by the arms of proud doctors. It was all over so quickly. Before mother had a chance to run a replay through her brain, baby was on the weighing scales like a supermarket delicacy. Label round its ankle with its surname on and an injection in the foot. Wrapped up in green it was handed this way and that, having various procedures carried out on it. To check that it really was a baby. A healthy one. The mother turned her head this way and that following her little prize round the room, pinned to the operating table by a green mountain of machinery, the light bathing her bleeding stomach in health glare. It was theatre all right. The mother crying, the baby crying, the nurses laughing at its squashed-up nose and wrinkled toes. I was awed. No matter how many babies I greeted this way, the theatre of it all always awed me.

But the terminations got to me. In, out. In, out. One after the other. Day in, day out. Day in, day out. After three days of Termination 4 Theatre, I said *I* wanted out. I wouldn't do it any more. I was a Catholic. I was against termination. Some of them actually *looked* pregnant. I felt really sick when the suction was turned on and the glass bottle slowly filled up with bits of baby. I just couldn't hack that so I made a stand. I was earmarked as a troublemaker. As a git. As the nurse with the big gob and the chip on her shoulder. So I made a bigger stand and was vilified for it. I was the anti-abortion queen of Mitton Hospital.

'It's murder. It's murder.'

'It's personal. You can't judge other people.'

'I can. It's murder. Every child sucked out is murdered. There's no other word for it. I'm not having any part of it.'

A robotic reaction from childhood. I was told that abortion was wrong, means-tested benefits were wrong, euthanasia was wrong, and shitting on your own doorstep was wrong. I didn't want to see bottled babies day in, day out so I screamed religion. Other Catholic nurses said they wouldn't do it, but none shouted it from the rooftops and ruined a good night down the pub like I did. Freedom. The mother's choice. Personal choice. Don't judge. What do you know about having kids? I answered them all with murder. Like a mantra. Murder. Stirred up – murder. From the moment of conception – murder. Doctors of death. Murderers. God was on my side.

Luckily, there was a variety of entertainment on offer in theatre. Women having their breasts enlarged. 'Mammary augmentation.' They came in with a 32-inch bra or no bra at all and brought a boxed 36-inch with them. At the end of the op, we all stood around admiring their new heaped mounds, knocking them hard, like the last of the workmen on the factory conveyor belt of new tits.

The women were still asleep. If they knew what went on . . . especially the attractive ones . . . Well, I saw doctors fighting to treat them. Pulling straws. Just so they could see their breasts. Feel them. Under the guise of a stethoscopic enquiry. They helped them to get better but they wanted to perve as well.

And car-crash victims. Some of them were tidied up a treat. It was like darning socks, pulling bits of skin this way and that. Trying to make a neat triangular flap to be sown into a square. Neat. Using thread that can barely be seen. Only the thinnest thread looks good. Doesn't leave much of a scar then. Some surgeons use a fat thread so they can get the job done. That's like sowing up silk with string. Not good.

Saturday nights were for the brawlers – getting their ears and noses sewed back on. There was an emergency theatre for that since it was a local custom. Biting off ears and noses.

As was playing music during operations. From Pink Floyd to Mahler. The surgeons competed with one another. To see who could act the most mad. The most eccentric. The most entertaining. One surgeon was particularly amusing when he did nose jobs on the NHS patients. Once the patient was asleep, the music went on. Der Der Der Derrrrrrrrrrrr, Der Der Der Derrrrrrrrrrrr, and then an almighty blow with a hammer right on the napper, just between the eyes. Looked ever so painful. We laughed. I could see the bruises climbing up from the neck waiting to settle in. The surgeon said most of the noses he did couldn't be improved because of the fizzogs behind them. On some of them I had to agree with him.

*   *   *

161

I waited patiently for a chance to be scrub nurse but I was every day consigned to do the cleaning. A lot of cleaning goes on in theatres and the cleaning is mind-bogglingly boring because theatre is always clean. OK, a few drops of blood maybe, round the operating table, and an odd bit of gauze on the floor. But the rest. The walls, the chairs, the sinks, the ceiling. All of it for the most part was clean. I had to imagine that all the surfaces were crawling with infectious bacteria too small for the eye to see. And so, day in, day out, cleaning.

Watching legs getting sawn off was a bit too close for comfort but these things have to be done. I was always surprised the patient didn't wake up. Then I really admired the anaesthetist. On your head be it, I used to think. Glad it's not me. I don't think the surgeons liked doing amputations because it was quite strenuous. Hard work. Graft. Sweat. A man with a red bag used to come and collect all the legs and arms and take them away to be burnt in the incinerator which had a chimney taller than the rest of the hospital. I used to wonder what else the man did. For the rest of the day.

In the evenings I lay in my bed and learned the names of instruments, sizes of scalpels, different thread thicknesses, retractors – great wedges on steel sticks to hold back all the skin so the surgeon can delve in and investigate, or remove or add to. Laparotomies use the biggest retractors. Holding back guts and all. They did lots of laparotomies. Slitting the body down the abdomen from the bottom of the chest to the top of the pubes. Exploratory laparotomies – when they didn't have a clue what was wrong so they opened them up to take a look.

Last resort it ought to be, but if there were new doctors around, then the EL numbers shot up. For practice, the appendix got removed. Just as a precaution. As a diagnosis they wrote 'spastic colon' which meant there was absolutely nothing wrong. But at least the diagnosis box on the form wasn't left empty. It's an awful lot of pain to go through only to read that the final diagnosis is a blank.

Very often the surgeons found things inside the body that they really weren't expecting. When they told the patient that they'd found something, the patient often died the next day or within the week – as if cursed by a witch doctor. It's surprising how downhill a patient can go when they know the truth.

One night, there was loads of blood. Because blood is thicker than water I thought it should contain itself better. Be more compact. But colour deceives. Well, red does. A pint of bright-red blood, oxygenated blood, bleeds further across the eye than a pint of water. And looks very alarming. This particular night we were drenched in blood so there was lots of cleaning. An emergency admission. A man threw himself out of a window from the second floor of a block of flats and landed on his head. He was running away from his probation officer. There was masses of pressure build-up in his brain and he needed 'bare-hole' drainage, urgently. There wasn't a surgeon on duty that night who knew how to do burrhole drainage so they rang someone up at Fazakerley Hospital and got them to direct the operation over the phone. But the phone wasn't in the operating theatre – it was outside – so someone had to stand by the phone and shout directions.

His head was shaved and two nurses and a surgeon were scrubbed up and at the ready with a Black & Decker lookalike, all within the space of five minutes. It was amazing. The head was covered with pen marks. Little black squares in black felt-tip.

The nurse outside shouted 'Left four and then right at intersection six' and other equally imprecise directions. Imprecise because the black felt-tip was dripping across his head in the heat and the sweat. At the intersections the drill went in. Brrrrrrrrrrrrrrrrrr! Blood spurted out of the head in jets. Squirts and squirts of it in all directions. The theatre, surgeon, anaesthetist, nurses – drenched in blood. The lights dripped with it. The floor awash. The excitement. My little legs jellied. Funny things go through the mind at midnight wiping up pints of blood – making it look like nothing ever happened. I didn't mind the cleaning then. There was a purpose to it. The man died. We did what we could. In a manner of speaking.

After taking the anti-abortion stance, I was consigned to ear, nose and throat theatre. More cleaning and no blood. No blood at all. Soul-destroying. I prayed for tonsillectomies to go wrong, every time, but they never did.

The sister in charge – Annie, everyone called her – hated me. I couldn't call her Annie. I had to call her Sister Bryce. She was another National Fronter. The place could have been crawling with them. Like cockroaches. Taking trolleys from theatre in the middle of the night, I saw all the cockroaches come out to play by the heaters. Hundreds of them. In formation, some of them. Crunching.

'What are you doin' in here?'

I was having my coffee on my break. My first day on ear, nose and throat. ENT, as they called it.

'Coffee?' I asked, explained, held up in my left hand to confirm I was telling the truth.

'Who said you could take coffee in here? I say who takes coffee in here.'

The other nurses sat with their heads down. Not speaking up for me. Not saying anything.

'Eh, Nurse Thompson. Did you hear me say that O'Leary could use this rest room?'

'No, Annie.'

I was still holding my coffee cup up, looking at Thompson then back at Annie and the heads of all the other nurses breaking their fast with biscuits. Nibbling slowly.

'So, O'Leary, what are yer doin' here?'

'Well, I thought this is where you take a break.'

'Well, it is if you've got permission.'

'I didn't know I had to get permission.'

'Well, you know now.'

'Where else can I go?'

'Back down to the other theatres. That's where you normally take your break, isn't it?'

'But then I'll have to get changed and . . .'

'Don't tell me your problems. Just go.'

She was laughing. No one else was. I was confused. She was making more a fool of herself than of me and I felt the other nurses agree with me. Their eyes went up in their sockets to tell me.

165

I put my cup down on the sink. I was slow. I thought about speaking up. Saying 'Why me?' But my scaredy-babby head wouldn't let me. Not when she'd given herself such a spotlight on the stage. No good would come of it.

As I was going through the palaver of putting a gown on and plastic bags over my shoes, she told me anyway. She told me why I had to go.

'Who yer voting for, Thompson?'

'Errh . . . I don't know yet – probably Margaret Thatcher.'

'What good's she gonna do . . . a woman . . . too soft. I'm voting National Front.' She said the last part really loud.

Then I didn't feel too bad. It wasn't like it was personal. It wasn't me she couldn't stand. Just the colour of my skin. That made me feel better. I could understand why she was how she was.

It took me ten minutes to dress up and ten minutes to walk there and back to the big theatres on the other side. When I got there the reception party was somewhat embarrassed to have me in their midst, since they all thought they'd got rid of me. The theatre sisters made slits out of their eyes when they saw me. I thought they were really scary. And then I was late back. I got bollocked every time I went down to the other theatres because I was always late back. In the end I just stood in the corridor outside ENT and waited until I was allowed back in. Thompson said she was sorry.

More cider.

The book didn't help. Kevin's book. *This Is Your Society*. I was unimportant. I was a tax payer. I was a consumer. I was a worker. I was overpopulating the planet at an exponential rate and soon the earth's resources would not be able to cope with me any more. I was powerless. It said what I was thinking and, because it was in print, it meant it was true. My witch doctor.

Chapter 18

More Cider.

'Who'd yer vote for?'

Sylvie was back from the polling station.

'Margaret Thatcher.'

'What?'

'Thatcher.'

'But why?'

'Coz she's a woman.'

'So what? She's a fuckin' Tory. No! She's worse than a fuckin' Tory.'

'She'll do things for women, won't she? She'll help nurses, won't she?'

'Bollocks.'

My first row with Sylvie. In my book, anybody with a brain voted Labour. Tories looked after the rich and Labour looked after the poor. It was simple. How could she have been so stupid?

She had popped her head round my door to say hello, mouth full of hairgrips. From wide-eyed shock of the assault her face narrowed, eyes slit. Hair grips gripped between lips zipped. I wasn't who she thought I was. I was someone else.

Drunk, I riled up at her just to get the message across. To show her the real me.

'You prat. You fuckin' prat.'

I wanted to chin her. There was her chin. Stuck round the side of my door, begging for it. She wasn't the person I thought she was. That person wouldn't have voted Tory.

'Piss off, you. Who the fuck d'yer think you are? Yer can't tell me how to vote. If I want to vote Tory then I will. What's it to you? Going into politics now, are we? You and your fancy books.'

She went home. I was mad jealous of that bike of hers. And that home of hers.

I shut the door all the time after that. I didn't want to see stupid heads popping round the side of it. Knocking and then popping. No more of that.

More cider.

I moved on to female orthopaedic. Nursing all the women I saw in theatre having their bloody hips replaced. I could tell a Thompson's a mile off. Yellow bruised legs with butcher's hacks in the thigh, wasted. Tom and Jerry cheese slabs between their legs to keep them straight and apart in the bed. Their legs Ordnance Survey maps with great big train tracks running down the side. Their pain. I couldn't get my head round their pain. It didn't matter. Of course it hurt. But how many times can you bow down to someone's agony? In a day. Not many. You have to brush past it. Recognise it, ignore it and then make them walk on it.

In theatre I saw the middles of thigh bones being scraped out and metal sticks with balls on the end put inside them. Then the ball clicking into the pelvic hip. Not dissimilar to snapping the leg back on a plastic doll. Except for the pain after. And then the leg was sown up quick. With gut. So much sewing to do, the surgeons couldn't fanny about with silk. Flesh closed up with a cat-gut zip.

I couldn't get my head round all that pain. Well, I felt responsible for it somehow. I'd participated in creating it.

Half of them couldn't walk properly before they broke their hip. That was why they'd broken their hip. A lot of them didn't want to walk after. The game was up. They wanted to sit and watch telly in peace till they died. But we had to get them up – get them at it again. Zimmer.

The therapists did some of the work but we were left with the day to day – the 'Get them to walk to the toilet'. A lot of them gave up and just pissed and shat in their bed. Others screamed in agony at the trying. I wanted to keep them in bed. I preferred to clean up their shit than listen to that agony.

I let some of them shit in peace. If they asked me, I had to take them to the toilet. They couldn't have a bedpan. They had to go to the toilet and after that go home. It's a hard life. Right to the end.

When a PE teacher came in with a knee injury needing an operation, I had Liam Cotswold and Charlie Fox in the office, arguing about who was going to book her in. She was trim. I looked at Foxy in disgust. He laughed at me. Said he was only kidding. He wasn't the sort to look at the patients as sex objects. He said.

'Yeah. Looks like it.'

'I'm not.'

'Then get a woman doctor up and prove it.'

Liam moaned.

'Why do you have to spoil everything?'

'She's right though. We shouldn't talk about stuff like that in front of her.'

'Thank you,' I said, smiling at him.

I liked him and I could tell he liked me. Not like that. I mean . . . as a nurse. Professionally.

The women on traction. What a laugh. Traction. OK. Some of them were in a bad way but a lot of them never helped themselves. They were supposed to lie flat. So they sat up to put their make-up on before hubby came in. Their beds were slanted in a special way and two weights hung from their legs over the end of the bed – the balance measured with precision. The traction was supposed to stretch the spine to bring a prolapsed vertebral disc back in line with all the others. Every time they sat up and put their make-up on, they added another two weeks on to their stay.

I was tempted to pull on the weights hard. To drag them down the bed in agony. To remind them of why they were in there. They were in there for months, some of them. Bored out of their skulls.

And the water beds. God, yes! The water beds. Ivana. Ivana Pelczynska. It took a while to notice that Ivana was actually in her water bed, it so high, wide, long, and she so small. Like a vat. Pipes up the side kept the water circulating and controls like those from *Voyage to the Bottom of the Sea* buzzed barometric dials at her feet. There was another bigger dial right next to her head.

We had to control the temperature and the water pressure. High pressure made the bed rock hard, like a full-on lilo. Low pressure made the patient disappear. That's why we didn't see Ivana most of the time. The pressure was put on low for her. She had pressure sores in her backside the size of caves. And that black too.

Besides two broken hips, Ivana suffered from paranoid schizophrenia. Ivana. She was wonderful. A doll. Little head with short white hair and eyes the size of clocks, always open wide. No teeth. She was all white. Hair, eyes, legs in a great big bed that was – all white. She didn't need a green counterpane, the water boiled her blood all day long.

Ivana took to shouting out, day and night, to people who weren't there.

'Tell the train to go,' she'd shout. 'Lock him up now, lock him up now.'

She stared straight ahead to a white ceiling. She couldn't sit up, the water wouldn't let her. Nor her legs which were wedged into a 'V' shape. All day and night she stared at the ceiling, talking and shouting at her past.

When they come in like that, yelling, railing against the institutionalised calm, when . . . well, then it's always good to know something of their past. I sat in the office, drank cocoa, and took a look at her medical history. Ivana had a history. Ivana was history. Her file was thicker than all the other patients' files put together. A Polish Jew, she'd worked for the French Resistance during the war. She had two sons. Her husband was captured by the Germans, she was told. She never found out for certain.

Her paranoid attacks were brought on by the sound of men's voices and the radio. When she heard the radio, she fitted and screamed at her imaginary Gestapo. Having helped to free France she came to England for some freedom of her own. When the kids grew up they were free to go to Canada. After they left, Ivana was free to eat what she wanted and she ate rice pudding. That's all. Just rice pudding. And that's pretty much what came out the other end.

A young doctor, intrigued by her psychiatric condition, decided he would put the woman to the test, to see if she really did respond to a radio. I couldn't stop myself. I had to. He was laughing at her. She writhed in her water torture like a maimed cat. And he was laughing at her. Her automatic response. His experiment.

I never got into trouble either. It's not done to drag a doctor off the ward. Thumping with tired fists. Screaming. You bastard. You bastard. You bastard. And that got me thinking about that war. And what Ivana thought about winning it.

And then it was back to traction.

'Nurse, have you got any magazines yer don't want?'

'Nurse, can yer pass the phone, please?'

'Nurse, is there any chance of more tea?'

'Nurse, my bum's sore. Could you come and give it a rub?'

'Nurse, me feet are itching.'

'Nurse, can I go to the toilet?'

'Nurse, can yer pass me my mirror?'

'Nurse, can yer put me flowers straight?'

'Nurse . . . nurse . . . nurse . . .'

Day in. Day out.

I took more and more time off work. In my room. Sylvie spent more and more time at home. Coming in on her bike

173

just before her shift started. I didn't even check her any more. I stayed in. Curtains closed all day. Food – toast. Drink – cider. Listen – Bob Dylan. 'There's a Slow Train Comin'.'

Chapter 19

New skin. Pink skin. Unwrinkled. Small beds and faces. Pictures on the walls. Dead babies.

On the first day of paediatrics a baby died. Cystic fibrosis. Daniel was his name. I saw him in the morning. In the afternoon he was dead. The parents looked like they'd been smacked round the neck with an iron girder. Bent. For ever bent. Parents of dead children. Their faces walk the middle of the air. Not on the ground. Not face to face. Somewhere in the middle, looking down. Their grief separates them from their body so they appear transparent like the uncooked white of an egg gone bad. Nothing solid. The fluid of life running through them like transfusioned blood. And death. Life and death running through at the same time. Bent in suspense. Their faces real. Their spirit held in a grip. These were people from a different place. Each noise cracked a bone. Each voice plucked a nerve. Each thud forewarned of life outside the baby's crib. They too wanted to be dead. In the crib. Bending over it. Trying to get inside it. Just to crawl inside with the baby and never come out. Their own wretched bodies still pumped with blood, guilt blood, evil blood, whilst their baby, white and dead, is taken and gone and so very small.

Sister Comfly wouldn't let me see the dead baby. Said it wasn't right. Never let any students see a dead baby. I wanted to see what it looked like. I wanted to feel if it was heavier than a live baby. I wanted to see its eyes.

There were quite a few spina bifida kids in. Huge heads and little bodies. And a fear in their eyes. Fear for the future, it looked like. The next minute. Month. Mither. Every now and again they came in to get their plumbing sorted out. Get their heads drained. Hydrocephalus. Water on the brain. They had little pipes above the ear draining the brain. The child hoping its head would get smaller.

There was one girl, Lizzie. She was fifteen. She shouldn't have been on the kids' ward really. She was massive. Huge head. She had plumbing problems down below as well. The other kids took the piss out of her. She wore disposable nappies so's not to mess up when there was an overflow. We used to do her bladder control for her. That was really amazing.

Biffo time, we used to call it. Now Sister Comfly didn't like us calling them biffos but I thought it was a great name and so did the biffos. When we took off Lizzie's boots, great red boots, just like Doc Martens only better, underneath where the size is usually stamped was the trademark. They were called Biffabout Boots. Even Lizzie laughed at that. So, at biffo time we went round and did the bladders. Pressing on the hard distended bladder, the same way as on a heart for resuscitating. Press hard down. When we pressed down, the piss shot out of her wee-hole straight into the bedpan. Fantastic. It was like emptying a hot-water bottle. I'd rather have that done to me any day – than be catheterised.

176

Like most spina bifidas, Lizzie was *compos mentis*. She had sexual feelings, heart-throbs and a bad temper. She knew how undesirable she was. I liked her a lot because she told me I had really lovely hands and I always thought my chocolate fingers fat and stumpy. I've always liked my hands since she said that. I have to look at my hands every day and she made me see them differently. Poor Lizzie. She had the most beautiful hands. Innocent, gentle, wanting hands. One day I cried for her, with her. We both sat on the bed and cried for her.

I thought nursing the kids would be fun. But it was hell. Or on the way there anyway. I hated the parents. I hated them when they cared too much and I hated them when they didn't care at all. The non-accidental injuries. Battered babies. Fag-burned babies. The most beautiful children with fag burns all over their arms and legs. And their mothers coming in screaming and shouting to get them back again. Calling the odds. I could have ripped their heads off. The mothers, I mean.

And the FTs. The failure-to-thrives. Tiny babies that wouldn't take their bottle. Wouldn't play life. Didn't want to join in. Stroppy bastards. It could take up to four hours to feed a single bottle and then the little animal spewed it all back up again. I sat whole shifts feeding one baby in between the yarling and the spewing and runny green stench of its shitting.

I was nursing an FT when I sensed evil for the very first time. The FT of FTs. It was screaming in my face. But like a laugh, not a sadness. Not a wanting. A ridiculing laugh. It stared at me from its black eggy eyes. Peep-hole eyes. Winking at me. I swear the creature was winking. Evil wink. The baby was saying something to me. It understood

177

my every thought. It had wisdom. It silenced itself to take some breath, to gather up venom, throw the wink, and then it laughed its head off all over again.

I paced up and down by the windows. In between trying to put the teat in its mouth I was trying to figure out how to open the window catches. Then I got one open. I put my head out of the window to see what the bilious little monster would land on if I threw it out. A parked car.

There was something else. Something the baby knew and I didn't.

'Hey, guess what? They've got a notice up in theatre saying that any nurse . . .'

'Ever 'eard of knocking?' Freda. Fast and forward Freda.

'Sorry.'

Whore, she was. Just walking in my kitchen, our kitchen, my space. She'd had a few abortions, I knew. Tart. I prompted her to continue.

'Saying that any nurse . . .'

She stopped. She was thinking about not telling me. Then she changed her mind.

'Saying that any nurse who doesn't want to do Termination 4 doesn't have to.'

'Wow,' sarcastically.

'I thought you'd be pleased. You're the one that kicked up all the shit about it. All the Catholics are grinnin' their 'eads off. The allocation officer's doin' his nut. He's gotta change all the rotas round. Must be murder doin' that, eh?'

A piece of toast I'd just buttered fell to the floor. It landed buttered side down. Coz the Pope's a Catholic.

'You been off sick again?'

178

She was getting on me nerves and the butter was all gone.

'Yep.'

'What's wrong with yer this time? You're always off sick!'

'Fuck off.'

'Yer shouldn't have such a chip on yer shoulder – sittin' around here feelin' all sorry for yerself. Take a look on the bright side for a change.' Said with sincerity sucking a Tip-Top.

'Fuck off.'

I left her stood in the kitchen, went to my room and banged my door shut.

In my room, I liked to think that I was a million miles away from the pain and the dying across the road, on the other side of the bridge that joined my home to the suffering. The green-and-yellow-striped plastic corrugated bridge through which, only just, the shapes of the cars beneath could be fancied. Encased in that plastic journey to work, I had only to tread a hundred steps to enter the bowels of human suffering. It took less than five minutes to reach a bed rank with piss and shit, from the opening of my eyelid and a coffee cup of bliss. So I stayed in my room.

The room was dark. Three rows of brown cider bottles turned it into a toilet. It smelt like a toilet. A mountain of clothes, jeans and nurse uniforms climbed up the sink. The cape I once loved hung on the back of the door like a matron choked. Dust. Three plates of crumbs and knives on top of one another. Two mugs of mouldy coffee waste next to them. A spilt ashtray. Brown fag ends. Silver ash. Used light bulbs brown. A poster of Che Guevara fallen, hanging by one corner of excess Blu-Tack. One body face down on the bed. At home. And who the fuck was Che Guevara anyway?

I wanted to be an FT. Stop taking part. Taking shit. I wanted to stay in my room.

Catholics came to pat me on the back, knocking on my door. Patting me on my back because they were no longer required to assist in the aborting of foetuses day in and day out. 'Well done.' 'Should have been done years ago.' 'God bless yer.' Patting me on my back. Knocking on my door.

I wondered how they'd take to me throwing real live babies out of the window.

More cider.

I couldn't make sense of them all. Why were they so happy? Why didn't they question the lives they were saving? Kevin did. I did. But the rest? They worked, played, fucked and drank. And slept. And to them that was life and they were going to carry on doing it until it was death. Why was I put on this earth? My body – one out of millions of bodies. A body that has legs and arms like a rabbit or a goat or a cow. Was I to reproduce like a dog? Was I to work like a mule? Was I to bow down to my masters and do what I was told? Find a husband, get a house, have kids, work and work and worry and work and drink and fuck and play a little bit and give birth and work and work and sleep.

My so called friends have fallen under a spell.

After paediatrics came anti-depressants before treading the bridge and over to geriatrics. Kevin had already done geriatrics. I asked him how bad it really was.

'It's enough to push you over the edge.'

'How come you're still here?'

'Well, I 'ad a bit of a struggle. And not coz o' the smell o' piss down there. Yer can smell that piss a mile off. Even the main entrance. No wonder no one visits the poor bastards. You wait. It smells like they mop the place with piss, honest. The piss just clings to everything. All patients piss but down the block . . . well, I don't know . . . can't figure it out. Anyway, if that wasn't enough, when I got down to Blossoms, guess who was workin' there.'

I was looking for some money. We were going down the pub. The anti-depressants were kickin' in a bit and I felt remote enough to take my chances and go out. Each swing door we went through, on our way out of the home, Kevin held back for me. I walked through the corridors with my head up, hating everyone and every door I walked past. Every door I walked through was a block in my brain being unplugged. Till I hit the air of the street. Out. The hospital glared back at me with its lantern-eye windows lighting up in sequence the floors of the building. It was just getting dark.

'No, I can't guess. Oh hang on. Bridget.'

'No. Arnie. He lives in the same house as Tokyo Joe. He's a right bastard. An absolute twat. I felt so sorry for the gerries, I really did. I felt I 'ad a duty to protect 'em if I could. D'yer know?'

No, I didn't know. I was in self-protection mode.

'He gave me a reason to stick at it, if yer like, coz he treats 'em like shit.'

'Did he say owt to yer? About Tokyo Joe, I mean?'

'Nope.'

'Good.'

'He didn't connect. Well, not until the last night. Then Tokyo Joe came down to the ward for somat. I think it was for some o' that mist. euphoria stuff. Yer know, the cocktail stuff for the ones that are on the way out. Coz as soon as Toke was in the ward, Arnie went straight over to the medicine trolley and swapped all the bottles around.'

'Yer didn't report him, did yer?'

'Fuck off! Well, I was going to and then Tokyo Joe saw me, recognised me like, so I figured we were quits then. If I don't tell on him for that, then I'm safe. If he does anythin' to me then he's not safe.'

'What makes yer think yer weren't safe?'

'Bridget. She said he was on to me. Told me to keep me nose clean.'

'And the medicine? What did he put in the bottle? Water?'

'Yeah.'

'So did yer start dishin' out water instead of euphoria? Yer didn't?'

'No. I smashed the bottle on the floor. I did it in front of Arnie so he witnessed and signed for it. He was a bit angry, I reckon, but I wanted to make sure whoever had to have it got some. The proper stuff like.'

'That's what I could do with, yer know? Some mist euphoria. It sounds great.'

'Don't talk soft. Anyway, now he knows I know. Arnie, I mean. In the morning when Sister came on she said it was the second bottle smashed in two weeks. I think she could tell somat was up. I'm glad I'm off that ward anyway. He gave me the creeps. What ward are you going on?'

'Tulip.'

'Oh you'll be all right then. Tulip is . . . mmm . . .

oh yeah, that's Gavin. He's in charge on nights. He's Indian.'

'From India?'

'Are yer takin' the piss?'

'No. I just wondered.'

'He's all right, Gavin. He has a laugh. I worked with him a couple o' nights. Oh by the way, I saw Bridget today.'

'Yer not still 'avin' a go?'

'Well, not so's she'd notice. I mean . . . well, I know her shift routines. I stand on the bridge to catch her going on and off. All last week, coz I was on nights and she was on earlys, I made sure I got off early so I could be there on the bridge when she came over. She looks brilliant then. In the mornin', I mean.'

'And does she talk to yer?'

'Sometimes. Well, she nods.'

'Noddin's not much good, Kevin. If yer think you've got a chance coz she nods at yer . . .'

'Easy does it, I say. All good things come to those . . .'

'But I don't think she's good, Kevin. Yer must know that by now.'

'Well, I realise she's a bit of a flirt but she's not going with Tokyo Joe any more so I'm in with a chance, and when I was with her before she said . . . well, she did say that I was different.'

The expression on my face told him what I thought about that.

'She didn't *just* say different. She said loads of other things as well.'

'Oh leave it out, Kevin, will yer? Different! Different!' I was squealing at him. 'She's fuckin' right! You're mental. She's never 'ad anyone like you before. Most blokes

183

are in and out. And here you are . . . You're different, all right.'

I could tell he was pleased we'd reached the pub. He didn't have the words or the courage to go on any more. To come back at me.

In the pub there was a mini disco going on. As I pushed against the heavy swing doors I could see them all oops-upside-their-headin'. I wasn't as anti-depressed as I thought I was. When I saw the thighs of the nurses with their skirts hitched up round their backsides, sitting on the floor, pretendin' to be rowing a canoe together, oops-upside-their-headin', when I saw that *that* was what I was supposed to be like, what I was supposed to be doin', what I was trying to be anti-depressed for, it made the whole idea of anti-depressants seem ludicrous. Sat alongside this theatre, my head down, I was a patient not wanting therapy.

Walking home, I was captured in another dream. A real dream. A wonderful dream. Until Kevin butted in.

'He was in there.'

'Who was in there?'

'Tokyo Joe. He was in there. With Bridget. I couldn't take me eyes off her.'

'What?'

'Tokyo Joe with Bridget . . .'

I snapped out of my dream. I gave it to him straight.

'Jesus, Kevin! I'm sick of it. Get Bridget off your fuckin' brain, will yer? It's over. It never began. She's a fuckin' whore. Forget her. Get your act together.'

He didn't come back with anything. Just a blank. I gave him some normal, to try to make it more right between us.

184

'What about Foxy then, eh, eh?' Nudging him. 'Never left my side all night. And guess what?' I suppose I was a bit insensitive really.

It had been raining. The air was squeaky clean, the car lights frazzling the night in a dazzle of red and white. Whoosh! Going places. Chattering. Drunk. I was part of it. Kevin didn't answer my 'guess what'.

Then a screech of a car. Kevin in the air. A rag doll landed in the road. I was annoyed. My happiness interrupted again. The car sped away, not stopping, not screeching, fast.

Someone stuck their head out of the window.

'I hope you've broke yer fuckin' neck, yer scabby little toe rag.'

It was Tokyo Joe. I was sure of it.

Kevin looked dead. He landed on his head. His glasses were smashed, lying in the kerb like a broken television. He was bent and disjointed, lying across the kerb. White against the tarmac. Some blood – oil in the night – leaked from the back of his head. Cars whooshed past. A couple of blokes appeared. They pulled him off the road and tried to straighten him out. I was off sick when they did first aid. Proper first aid. I didn't know where to begin. I wanted to run. My body was saying run and the faces of the men were waiting for me to do something.

'Are you a nurse, love?'

I didn't answer. I just stood there gormless. I could see the ambulances across the road. Sitting outside casualty.

Minutes later one turned up with two police cars. I was the only witness. The men said that. Then I heard a voice in my ear.

'Don't make a statement. Yer didn't see a thing.'

I don't know if the voice was real or whether I imagined

185

it. I heard it though. I didn't turn round to see who said it. Dazed. Death and lights and noise made my stomach full. I spewed up. I thought of Mrs Duncan. I wished I could have done it like her. Projectile. Instead, the vomit feebly cascaded in weak bursts out of my mouth on to my shoes and the pavement.

I was taken to casualty and treated for shock. That meant being sat down and given a cup of tea. The cobbler's shoes. I didn't want to be there. Last bloody place I wanted to be.

'Excuse me, miss, I realise how tired you must be, but we would like you to give us a statement. Could you come down to the police station in the morning?'

'It was Tokyo Joe. He did it. Well, he didn't do it coz he wasn't on the driver's side, but he was in the car.'

'And who the hell is Tokyo Joe when he's at home?'

And then the warning came in my ear again. That time I believed it. I didn't need to turn round. The cup of tea did the trick. It made me remember Kevin, Bridget, mist euphoria and a broken head on the pavement. My lips were sealed.

'Oh I don't know. I don't know if it *was* 'im – I'm a bit confused.'

Being confused is perfectly acceptable in hospital. Confused is the term nurses use to describe patients that are downright barking mad, belligerent or just a bloody nuisance. Confused people often get injections if they don't look out. I was confused enough to pervert the course of justice.

He made notes. I recognised him. He was going out with one of the nurses in our year. He was barely finished with Scouts, I reckoned, holding his notebook like a child on a nature walk. I said I'd be down there the very next morning. Except I wouldn't be.

Charlie Fox had organised that. Earlier in the pub.

'Found a penny and lost a quid?'

That was because he saw my face looking at the nurses, oops-upside-their-headin'. When I first got in there.

'Nah, I'm all right, actually. Nice to get out of the nurses' home.'

'I'm not having that. You look as miserable as sin.'

'Oh, and you're 'avin the time of your life, are yer, with this lot?'

'Well, as life goes, it's not too bad. I'm not suffering. There's a lot to be thankful for.'

'Jesus. Yer sound like a fuckin' priest. Yer missed your vocation.'

'Well, come on then. What's made your world so black? Sorry I . . .'

'What for? Sorry for what? I'm not with yer.'

'Black! I didn't mean . . .'

'Oh for Christ's sake! Is that all yer can see? Does the word black embarrass yer?'

'Oy, yoy yoy! Behave! There's no need for that. I meant no offence. I was trying to be funny. Jesus! What's with you? Take it easy . . .'

I made him raise his voice to me. Dr Ungettable Charlie Fox without his girlfriend, and there I was pumping shit in his face. Doin' a Duncan. The cage bars bent inwards. I should have stayed in my room where I was free. I should have stayed in. He was eyeballing me, waiting for me to say something meaningful.

187

'I'm on geriatrics tomorrow. Nights. Twelve weeks. I'm dreadin' it. The piss. Everything.'

'Let me get you a drink.'

Avoiding trite.

The disco went into full bump mode.

He started shouting in my ear.

'Do you want to come with me to Chester in the morning? In the MGB? I'm doing a bit of shopping and there's an open-air concert on the river. I'll get you back for eight?'

Asking me out. Asking me out. After I said yes I couldn't talk to him. I was full up. I never asked him about his occupational therapist.

So. I wasn't going to tell Dib Dib Dib all about that. I led him on and smiled in the right places, looked pained and strained and played wimpy victim for another five minutes and then ran back to the nurses' home in a half-panic, half-triumph. I threw up again all over the hallway. I shouldn't have got pissed on anti-depressants. Any nurse should know that. I couldn't stop crying when I finally lay down. I'd never done that before. Not as a grown-up. Never stop. Never stop. Never stop crying.

Sylvie knocked on my door.

'Can I come in?'

'Only if yer sleep with me.'

'Is Kevin dead?'

'No, unconscious.'

'Let us in then.'

It's such a perfect day . . .

Chapter 20

Should I look feminine or casual? Jeans or jupe? Make-up or straight up? I didn't know. I didn't ask Sylvie coz she would have got the idea that I considered the day out with Foxy a date. A proper date. I was sensible enough not to give that impression. In fact I told Sylvie that I asked him for a lift. Said I wanted to go to Chester to get clothes. And to see the place. Someone told me Chester was like a fairy town. I don't believe in fairy-tales. Never have and never will. Happy ever after wasn't in the script.

Getting clothes was a good ruse. Being depressed made me lose weight. I was less than nine stone. The clothes I had hung off me so deciding on what to wear on this very important occasion was unbelievably time-consuming. Having got Sylvie out of my room, I emptied every drawer and even the washing basket searching for anything that would at least do. I did casual in the end.

When I got to the porch of the nurses' home I saw him there ready, engine running, hood down and a smile for me to catch when he saw me. We never spoke. I felt so low down in the car I worried about the floor being safe. I imagined my bum scraping along the road all the way to Chester. I remembered Dad's Lecky van. I could see over people's hedges in that. I could look up their noses in an MGB.

He wasn't exactly casual. Well, he had jeans on and that, but he had a proper shirt on. No tie but a collar and cuffs job nevertheless. And a leather jacket that was too small for him. I asked him to put the hood up. I was freezing.

'So you don't want the wind in your hair?'

'Precisely,' I said.

'I didn't mean . . . it's supposed to be a good feeling having the wind blowing through your hair.'

'I'd rather wear a helmet.'

I think I was ruining things for him but I knew what he meant. Trouble was, with an Afro, if I went careering down the road with the wind in my hair, I knew I'd look like a black bottle-washer by the time we got to Chester. I wasn't chancing that.

After the hood was up I felt like Joe 90. He felt a bit cramped, I could tell. He smiled though to cover up what he was really feeling. Then in a great noise we burned our way to Chester.

He wanted to buy another leather jacket, one that fitted. He tried to get me to buy a long red velvet dress but I wasn't that stupid. Where on earth was I going to wear a long red velvet dress? 'But it looks wonderful,' he said in the shop. I wasn't asking him. We'd gone our separate ways in a big department store. Arranged to meet at the bottom in an hour. I only tried it on because it was velvet and cheap. He turned up when I was looking at myself. 'But it looks wonderful,' he said. That in itself was a warning.

I bought some jeans that fitted and I kept them on. Then I bought a couple of shirts that fitted – they were a bit on the feminine side. I wore one of those. And shoes. High shoes to make me look a bit taller. I did all that and he was still wandering around, looking for a leather jacket. He chose a really poncy one in the end. It was massive, purple, and had drawstrings dangling about all over the place. When he pulled them tight he looked like a duffel bag from behind. I felt ashamed walking alongside him. He had to wear it, of course. Walking up the streets you could see people looking at him. At us.

Then we went down to the river. It was ending summer and the throngs had been and gone. The chairs outside the cafés were mostly empty. We had jam and cream with scones and, whilst eating this, a really noisy brass band started tuning up on the bandstand.

'Is that the concert?'

I was choking on the glued-up scone stuck in the back of my throat. The thought of spending more than a second listening to uniforms playing trombones demoralised me. No matter how hard I tried I couldn't feign enjoyment at that.

'I'll go and check.'

He walked over there. I watched him trying to walk casually in his duffel bag. He looked all screwed up, chewed up. His hair was all over the place and thinning at the back. I'd never noticed that before. He had his hands in his pockets playing confident. I ordered more tea, the scone still choking me, making a blanket of cement across my tongue and my teeth. I saw him reading a noticeboard. He had to stand really close to read it, so he probably wore glasses when no one was looking. Everyone else reading the noticeboard stood behind him.

His girlfriend Julie (his fiancée when he corrected himself) was in Malta visiting her parents. Her father was in the Royal Marines. Charlie was at a loose end. He could see that I was at a loose end so he thought it a good idea if we were loose-ended together for the day. I was glad I never put any make-up on.

He walked back swinging his weight from one leg to the other, his hands buried deep in his pockets, his head and chin buried in his chest, like it was winter. He was trying to look knowledgeable. Confident again. I watched the swans and only turned to him when I heard his chair scrape against the pavement. He caught my nonchalance and recognised it as real. I could tell.

'I take it that *is* the concert?'

'Well, it wasn't supposed to be. There was supposed to be a real do with strings and a soprano, the Chester Chambers. Cried off, apparently. D'you fancy a boat trip?'

I thought about that for a second.

'What? On our own or one of those over there?'

'No, a little rower, on our own.'

'OK.'

He did everything. The rowing, the paying, the guiding and the talking. He didn't stop talking.

'So what about Kevin?'

'I didn't know yer knew.'

'Well, I heard something.'

'What about him?'

'Is he all right?'

'Concussed. Broken arm. Few ribs. Nothin' too serious.'

'Who did it?'

'Leave me out, Sherlock.'

'I was just asking.'

'How would I know?'

'But you do.'

Telling me I do.

'Do I?'

'Well, I reckon so.'

'Well, you're wrong. Stick to bodies, Dr Fox.'

'Hey, there's no need to get shirty.'

'There's no need to interrogate me. What the fuck do I know?'

'Now you're getting mad.'

'Only coz . . .'

'Why are you being so aggressive? I'm only trying to help.'

'I thought you were at a loose end. Now you're a fuckin' social worker, are yer?'

'I'll shut up then.'

'Good idea.'

The mansions on the riverside were obscene. I saw servants in one of the gardens, all in pinnies, under some tarpaulin. Putting glasses on big long tables. Like I said, I don't believe in fairy-tales.

'Shall we go back?'

'Yeah. I'm cold. I don't like boats.'

'You should've said.'

'I didn't know. Never been in one before.'

'Well, not all boats are like this.'

'Never!'

'Listen. I didn't mean to get at you. Will you calm down a bit. I was only asking. I thought you and Kevin were close.'

'I'm not goin' out with him if that's what yer mean.'

'You can be close without going out with someone.'

'I know.'

I saw Smudger's face staring back at me when I looked under the water. I tried to imagine him treading the water in the canal, trying to swim, all the water tipping into his mouth, too much of it for him to spit out, and then I saw him sinking under the surface. I saw his little face staring back at me from under the boat and we left him there.

When Charlie pulled me out of the boat on to the quay, he took hold of the top of my arm and my stomach did jumps. I shivered at the sensation. Then walking back to the car-park he took hold of my hand and I couldn't understand. I wasn't his girlfriend, his fiancée. What was he saying to me? I didn't want to pull away.

He kissed me on the forehead before opening my side of the car. We both sank into a silent drive back to the hospital.

'Do you want to come to my flat for something to eat before going back to the home?'

'Mmm. OK.'

He did eggs and bacon and toast. And orange juice. Then he opened a bottle of wine. I still wasn't worried about Kevin. I knew he'd be OK. And anyway he'd been warned. It wasn't my fault.

Charlie told me to take my shoes off. Said they must be killing me. They weren't but I took them off anyway. When I sat up, finished with the shoes, he was behind me and his hands slipped inside my shirt. Then he began to undo the buttons. That's when everything went really mental. The insides of my legs, my stomach, my nipples, my common sense. He was rhythmic, breathing and rubbing in time, heavy. I just sat there and let all his madness roll over me.

He stood me up and then he sat down in my chair. He undid me all over and then sat there examining me. Touching me. Then he told me to lie down on his sheepskin rug that was in front of an electric fire, red-barred and blaring. Flat on my back, naked, him looking down on me, I felt like a baby. And then he went somewhere. To the bathroom, I think. I just lay there still, sucking my thumb because it felt right to do that. It felt OK.

When he came back he was half undressed. The bottom half. Smiling, he brought himself down to my level. Sniffing and smiling. I wasn't smiling. I was wondering. Then he got to work. I could see the picture of his fiancée on the mantelpiece. I was looking at her whilst he was doing it to me. She was stood next to a horse smiling. He stopped what he was doing to look at me. Then he told me to turn round. So he couldn't see my face. And I couldn't see hers.

'Better get you back. Back in time for duty.'

'Yeah. I wanna go and see Kevin as well. See how he is.'

'Right. Chop-chop. Better hurry in that case.' Like he was doing me a favour.

I didn't like the wine very much. He did. He gulped down mine and then poured himself another and drank half of that.

The nurses' home was in all its brutality after such a day. A day out. On the river. In his flat. His home. In the nurses' home there are no mornings or horizons. Just rooms and sinks and bathrooms and carpet and locked doors and open doors and tables and chairs and cupboards full of food for one. And keys and surfaces and uniforms and notes with rules on and lists and hair grips and pins and scissors and watches and tape and music and lights and shouts and screams and drink and women and signs and telephone rings.

With all that to brace against, to face and function in normal style, I remembered Foxy better than he was. Better. Rather than the shoes and shoelaces and stockings on radiators. The fences and paths that led to more doors and windows and fences with signs on and uniforms and women and doctors in white coats. There were glass doors that flew back so strong they didn't want you in there. There were locked doors and more locked doors and corridors long and wide with noticeboards and pictures of children on the tide with buckets and spades, in some other age, with curly blond hair and pantaloons.

There were noises that echoed all through the doors, and telephones that rang and rang and girls that cried for hours sitting on floors hanging on to phones in the corridors. There were wardens in white with pockets full of keys gliding down the stairs with smiles, controls, at home, at ease. There were clatters from the canteen, always feeding, night staff, day staff, eating carrots and peas and gravy and mince and stodge pudding with lumpy custard, knives and forks at the ready. So much of it.

It was later than I thought so I was just in time to get showered and changed and be on the ward for 8.00 p.m. It was a brilliant day even if Charlie Fox was not the man I thought he was. And when I thought of the river and being in the boat on our own, I remembered seeing Kevin's face under the water, not Smudger's.

'Hello. Yes, it's Nurse O'Leary from Tulip. I was just ringing to enquire about Kevin Riley. Have his parents been? Right. Yes. Sure. Good. Good . . . No, I'm sorry I can't come over till later. I'm on nights. I'll try and nip over on me break. Give him my best, won't yer?'

I was expecting Gavin the Indian to be in charge. I was looking forward to hearing all about India. Being in charge is no great shakes on geriatrics. The porters could take charge on geriatrics.

The sister going off handed the red cord and keys over to a man with white skin, no hat, no stripes, no belt and no badge even. He wasn't even an auxiliary. He was called a ward orderly. A fat toothless git of a ward orderly. He was the only ward orderly in England, someone told me. He had influence and bad breath. And grey greasy hair.

'This is Arnie, Nurse O'Leary. He's usually on Blossoms but Gavin decided to do a swap tonight. Yer can get him there if you need him. Yer shouldn't do. Not unless someone goes. Arnie knows this ward well enough anyway. He was on here for years before he moved over, so you're in good hands.'

'Why are yer givin' him the keys? I'm in charge, aren't I?'

'Yes, Nurse, but Arnie knows the doin's. No one knows these wards better than Arnie.'

'But . . .'

'Down here in geriatrics, Nurse . . . well, it's more like a cottage hospital. We're different from the rest of the hospital. The patients know Arnie. And they get confused if too many new faces start calling the odds so . . . just follow Arnie. He'll show yer what to do.'

Arnie was sat in the kitchen with his legs up on the table.

'First thing you can do, Nurse O'Leary, is to make me another cup o' tea and then yer can start the charts. There's not that many. We're not expectin' anyone to go tonight. Two sugars.'

'Bye, Arnie. Bye, Nurse O'Leary. Have a good night!'

Arnie got up and locked the door. That was the rule down in geriatrics because it was away from the main hospital and we just didn't know who was wandering about in the middle of the night. The Yorkshire Ripper was expanding his territory.

I made his tea in a pot and put the sugar on the table in a bowl. I expected him to come back, sit down and drink. Instead he came up behind me. He pulled my arms behind my back and put his big smelly face in the crick of my neck.

'Come with me.'

I with on auto-pilot.

The ward was getting dark. Only the small night-lights were on. I didn't want to follow him. I wanted to run but I couldn't. I just did as I was told. I just do as I am told. So I followed him – walking into trouble. Knowingly. He told me to bring a wheelchair. He went towards one of the patients in bed. He threw off the covers and picked the patient up. The patient didn't move a muscle. Bob. Worked down a pit. Used to. I was told about him. He'd been there for years. Social problem, they called him. He was famous for not liking Des O'Connor. Everyone played him Des O'Connor to get a reaction. Geriatrics was short on patients who could still remember how to give a reaction. Bob never moved a muscle. He could have been dead. Arnie fireman's-lifted him into the wheelchair. I moved away.

'Get back here or I'll fuckin' crucify yer.'

He was the hunchback of Notre-Dame, Arnie. His teeth. His build. His stoop. I wasn't that scared but the air under my nose told me that I should be. So I played at it. I should have been scared.

He wheeled Bob into the bathroom and I followed. Arnie turned the taps on and it was like listening to a huge waterfall, the rush of water in the airy bathroom, empty of everything, except us, the bath and a bathchair. Arnie went back to the door and locked it. The water-fall was all there was and you could've knocked me down with a feather if I didn't at that moment think of me playing cowboys and Indians at Butlin's. Being lassoed.

'Why yer lockin' the door?'

He ignored me.

The water woke Bob up. He looked around to see where he was. Checking if he'd died yet, it looked like. When he saw Arnie he went back to sleep again. As though Arnie could knock him out just by looking at him. Arnie took the old man's pyjamas off. Made me hold the wheelchair steady. The trouser bottoms were covered in shit. He must have been lying in it for ages. It stank worse than normal shit.

Why was Arnie being so melodramatic about a bath? I knew trouble was coming but I couldn't tell where from. The water filled the bath fast. Deep. The bath I always wanted. Why didn't he make *me* bath the man? Why didn't he go back to the kitchen and have his cup of tea? I was expecting Tokyo Joe to turn up any minute. Why didn't Arnie make me bath Bob? That was what I was there for. The dirty work. I didn't mind . . . honest.

199

He put the man on the chairlift and swung him over the bath. He lowered him in slowly. When Bob was submerged Arnie turned round quick to find me at the door, trying to get out. He pulled me away from it then slapped my back against it, his hand under my neck.

'Yer don't know who I am, do yer?'

'Arnie the Hulk?'

'Don't be funny. Where were yer?'

'When?'

'Today.'

'Chester.'

'Not down the copshop then?'

'Nope.'

'I know Tokyo Joe, yer know.'

'That's nice.'

'I know you know him too.'

'Well, I wouldn't say I . . .'

'I know what you know.'

'I don't know nothin', mate.'

'Did yer check your messages when yer got back from Chester?'

'No. I don't get messages.'

'Well yer do now.' Arnie fiddled in his pockets. Then he held up three 'while-you-were-out's. From the nick. 'They want yer to make a statement. *They* know yer know as well, don't they?'

'Look, Arnie. Don't worry about me. My lips are sealed. I've never grassed on anyone in me life.'

He put his hand across my mouth. It stank of Bob's shit.

'You bet yer fuckin' life they're sealed. I live with Joey

200

and the rest of the Hillings. There's loads of us. I'm not family but I'm treated as – just the same.'

At this point I could tell Arnie had been watching too many movies. Drunk on his power. His Bogart grimace was recognisable but idiotic. He was toothless except for one stray. I was in the wrong movie anyway. Had been since the very first day.

'Joey knows there's a witness but he doesn't know it's you. And I'm not gonna tell him.'

'Why not?'

'If they knew it was you they'd *do* you. Know what I mean? I mean they can't afford to risk it. Especially with you bein' a nigger an' all. They don't like niggers.'

'So how come you 'aven't told 'em?'

'Because . . .'

Bob slid down the bathchair. Arnie turned round and secured him better. That was my chance to leg it. And I blew it. I couldn't take it all in. Was he just giving me a warning?

He was back in my face.

'Because I want something from you. If I take it and you tell on me then . . . well, *then* I'll have to tell the whole family all about you. And the top brass 'ere won't frighten me half as much as . . . well, I think you know about the Hillings now, don't yer? Get over there by the chairlift.'

It was all sorted. I didn't look in his eyes. I knew what was there. I wasn't even scared then . . . when I knew what he was after.

I did as he told me. He came right up close. His breath clouded me in stench. He pressed his mouth against mine. That scared me. His heavy head pressing on my mouth,

201

hot wet spit mixing with mine, dribbling inside my lips. I couldn't swallow. I retched and my head fell forward suddenly, so he went for it again. He pushed me back against the chairlift. My feet were cemented. Like the weights on a netball post. Just cemented there with my sticky wobbly legs fit to snap, wavering about. The pole of the chairlift was digging into my back whilst Arnie pressed himself against me. I lifted my arms to push him off. He grabbed hold of both of them, shouting.

'Down,' he screamed, pulling them down to my side.

I was resigned then. He pulled at the press studs on my uniform. Starting from the top. I didn't look him in the face. My eyelids were down. As he pulled each press stud, I remembered the song, *Branded, and you know you're a man*.

Then he pulled the uniform to my shoulders and hung it there so that my chest was open to him. The smell of the shit from the pyjamas was solid air between us. So strong it overpowered his breath, his threat. His hand took a breast from my bra. He wiped the nipple as lipstick from the lips of a harlot wife. Then the same to the other and then to both. On his chest I saw sticking out of his pocket a label in a plastic bracelet, a patient's bracelet. It said, 'Arnold Warburton. Blossoms'. I thought about the shit smell.

Then he bent down towards my breast. To suck one of my tits, and as he bent down I realised that the bracelet sticking out of his top pocket was attached to a pair of scissors. I could hear Bob snoring. Bob and me were the same. We did as we were told. I looked for his scissors again. They were still there. Gary taught me

202

one thing. To fight. Not to give in. Not to give in. Fight. Fight. Dirty if I have to. I didn't fight Foxy. I couldn't. Him so sweet – what with his wine and his fire and his sheepskin rug. I couldn't fight that stuff. But this. Being manhandled by a greasy toothless git. Piece of piss. I looked for his scissors again. He was on my tit. The scissors were still there. He fiddled with his tunic to get at his pants. The label on his scissors begged me. 'Arnold Warburton. Blossoms.' I snatched the scissors and like D'Artagnan they were at his throat. His Adam's apple was bobbing at me. Waiting to be cored.

He was panting.

The scissor point was popping his skin. One wrong move. He backed off. Like a flash I was down to pick up the old man's pyjamas and then I threw them at his head, then rubbed them in so they were stuck to him. His face – covered in it. I had shit on my hands but I didn't give a ... I was out of there. I legged it down the ward. I couldn't unlock the door. Arnie had the key. I turned to see if he was on to me ... after me ... nothing. I went to the office. A sash window. I opened it and climbed out into the rain.

The next morning Dib Dib Dib was knocking my door down.

'I'm not makin' a fuckin' statement.' Screaming.

I requested another ward. I penned a really good letter, polite and professional. I explained that it wasn't that I wanted to avoid geriatrics, but that I wasn't ready for it and that perhaps a spell on the psychiatric wards would be just as beneficial and would still contribute towards my qualification.

A letter came back. Between the lines. 'Get back to work. No. There isn't another ward. You are listed for geriatrics and geriatrics it will be.'

The allocation officer wrote the letter himself. Between the lines. It said that I was the one who'd fucked about with his stupid jelly-bean timetable. I was the one that gee-ed up the Catholics. I was the one responsible for the chaos in the termination theatre. All his little coloured bars on his big allocation board had had to be rearranged. It was murder. He wasn't gonna be doing me any favours. And who did I think I was? Time I did something about that chip on my shoulder. Then back to the lines. He hoped that I would find myself fit enough to return to my allocated ward as soon as possible as excessive sickness could have, no, would have, a detrimental effect on my receiving any sort of qualification at all.

So I stayed off sick. On anti-depressants which I never took. I spent weeks lying in bed. Where it was safe. Telephone messages from Kevin were put under the door. Even the wardens tried to get me at it. Pretended to feel sorry for me. Sylvie, I completely ignored. She couldn't give me what I wanted.

Everyone on the landing was on nights. Everyone. Did the allocation officer do that too? Was I . . .? Was I . . .? Paranoid? Everyone on the landing got up at five in the afternoon, made a racket in the kitchen and drifted off into the hospital world. On their days off they drifted off home to their other lives. They knocked on my door but I pretended sleep. Or shouted OKs or go aways. I wouldn't let them in. I couldn't let them in. I didn't even look out to the ration of my sky. My room was a cave. And filthy.

And then I *was* sick. Day and night sick. I was pregnant.

Chapter 21

Cow stalls. We lined up in the shed, bumping into each other, our tits poking out of the paper-towel gowns we wore. We were shunted up one end and then back down the other. Clinical trolley tractors were pushed between us, in and out of us, and we all mooed at the commotion. There were at least thirty of us. Some girls complained out loud.

I stayed stumm. Blind, deaf and dumb.

In the hands of doctors, I'm stupid. No fuss. No delay. Knowing what can happen. I just lie back and think of. And abattoirs. When he says, 'Open wide,' I open wide. When he says, 'Relax,' I tense up. When he says, 'Relax,' again, I tense up even harder. He's getting angry. He's in a rush. He's got hundreds more to do. When he wants me to speak, I speak like a Jew going to the chamber. I speak calmly. Quiet. I don't give them any more work than they already have, else they'll take it out on me. When he asks, 'Does it hurt?' I say, 'No.'

They called my name. Date of last period. Date of last sex. Date of birth. Date of death to be given later. Come this way.

I lay on a trolley that moved when I got on it. Everything was temporary. The gloves. The gown. The paper cover. The sterility.

Put your legs in these. The stirrups. Stirrup. Stirrup. Lie there and wait. And wonder about the stirrups. And why I couldn't just open my legs. The missionary position.

There were at least twenty other stalls and each one could have had a woman lying inside with her legs in stirrups – naked. Waiting.

Eventually a doctor. A man in a white coat. No nurse. No woman.

Date of last period. Date of last sex. Date of birth. Date of death to be given later.

He put on a glove. Not aseptic. Like the man that unblocks the drains, he came alongside the trolley and stuck his middle finger right up me looking for something. He lifted the paper gown I was wearing and with his other hand, ungloved, felt me. When he was finished I pulled the gown over my body and he told me to move it back again. He reckoned I was less than six weeks. He would like his medical students to come and examine me. *He* pulled my gown back up for me. Exposing. Waiting.

Patients lie to their visitors. Their condition is so unusual half of Guy's Medical School come up from London just to take a look at their infested gall bladder. It's boring in hospital. I can't really blame them for lying. To entertain the visitors. To give the illness value. They're asleep before they go into theatre, asleep whilst they're in it and out for the count for a good eight hours after. There's nothing other than a scar and the pethidined pain. Some have got an amputated limb. And the splenectomies are jealous! What have they got? They dream up events instead. The needle as long as the biggest bass. The stitches count to the mourners at their funeral. Pints of blood to equal those drunk on their stag night. The nurses were sent from heaven and the doctors, though Bangladeshi, were of genius. Couldn't understand a bloody word they said but of genius.

Christ wasn't just born. He was born of a virgin mother. He didn't just die like a criminal. He came back to life again.

Lying stark naked in front of six young healthy medical students is one thing. Having each one finger you and feel you up is another. I let them do it. Keep the patient covered. Give the patient dignity. Reassure the patient. Reassure the patient. Be blind. Be deaf. Be dumb. Did they do that or did I just imagine it?

Was I . . .? Was I . . .?

Bob Dylan's anger carried along the corridor because I left the door to my room wide open. I didn't expect Sylvie to be in.

She was in. Her door was open. Hesitation. I didn't know whether to bother. Whether to bother telling her. What was it to do with her? What could she do? I never told her about Arnie. Why tell her about this? A baby. She'd want to know why I hadn't reported Arnie. Then she'd call me a coward. She'd say Kevin deserved more friendship than that. What did she know? She didn't understand. She thought it was a crime for parents to smack their fucking children.

'Have yer seen this?'

She was waving an envelope at me. She tossed it over but I let it fall to the floor.

'It's from Kevin. He's in Glasgow. Not coming back.

What shall I do with his get-well present? I was gonna post it to his mum.'

'What the fuck's he doin' in Glasgow?'

I was not surprised he'd gone away. After the Arnie incident, I received three letters telling me to do just that. Not to Glasgow though. Back to where I came from.

'I expect he thinks he'll be safe there.'

'Hardly.'

I had a sneaky suspicion that Glasgow was full of people like Arnie and Tokyo Joe. Kevin should have gone to somewhere calm, like the Lake District. Somewhere where there's lots of trees and water.

She was polishing her shoes. She never did that usually. Her mum did that.

'Sylvie, I'm pregnant.'

She looked up from her shoes but not shocked. She was hiding her shock or burying it so's to give some compassion. Maybe. She tossed her shoes aside and sat cross-legged on the floor. A wise Indian. She lit a fag and blew a tunnel of smoke. I took one of her fags and bit the end so hard the filter broke off. I went to get another and she put her hand on mine and I almost wanted to hug her but I couldn't. I couldn't let myself be hugged. I needed to stay strong.

I pulled my hand away, grabbed a fag and lit up like a tart. Sure.

'So you're leavin' then?' She was surprised at my low temperature. My machinery. 'Whose is it? Kevin's?'

'No, it's not Kevin's and I'm not leavin'. I'm gonna get rid of it.'

She smiled first.

'If Kevin offered to marry you, would you change your mind?'

'I don't wanna get married. I don't . . .'

'But d'yer love him or was it just . . .'

'Shut up! I'm gettin' rid of it. That's it! OK!'

'Yer've got some front, 'aven't yer?' Mocking. Deriding me. Repeating me. 'I'm gettin' rid of it.'

She was angry.

'What else can I do? I don't wannit. No one else'll wannit. Why should I make it live? Why?'

'Look, you!' She was yelling her head off. It felt good. The baby deserved it. Some yelling. Some life. Even if it was only this. Some emotion. Discussion. Something to remember it by. 'You don't need to tell me why people have abortions. *I* know. Suddenly you understand. Suddenly you've got ears, have yer?'

And I didn't feel like crying. Recognising the fact made me want to cry my eyes out but I was only sad I wasn't sadder. It would have been fake to cry under those circumstances. So I held off.

'I was wrong. I didn't know. I never thought, did I? I thought I believed but I don't. I don't believe in anything. Any more.'

I believe in you, even through the tears and the laughter . . .

She snarled the baby's life back up to me. Her lip turned it up so it had voice, reason, a shelf to sit on. Her eyes were downcast with mockery. Mockery of my Catholicism. Life sitting on her lip shelf. Cleaning her shoes, vigorous, self-assured. She spat on my Catholicism. I could spit on it too but in my way, in my time. She spat. And worse than that, she believed she was right. She was right to spit on Catholicism. Drag it to the back of her throat, collect up her resistance to its right

210

to be, right to act, right to wrong, and then with full force – spit.

She had iron faith. She sat, a Proddy dog from my schooldays, deriding me. Me the Catholic. A swift belt round the ear . . . but I was nineteen. I couldn't do that. It was wrong. Everything was wrong. Abortion. Was wrong. Catholics were wrong. The Sunday Mass, the Benediction, the Confession, the Confirmation, the Mothers' Union, the Lent, the Holy Days of Obligation, the Communion, the Genuflection, the Rosary, the Angelus, the Penance, the Everlasting Spirit. All fucking lies. Till Death Do Us Part. The Last Rites. The Original Sin. The Resurrection. Holy Water, cleanse me. All fucking lies.

I didn't believe. I never had believed.

Did Mary have an orgasm? Can perverted priests forgive? And who's the fuckin' Pope anyway?

Sylvie looked after me. She covered for me. She took me to Liverpool and helped me kill the baby.

It disappeared. Into a glass bottle. The bottle looks like a sweet jar. The kind I used to see when I was a kid – full of pineapple chunks down the corner shop.

My doctor at the nurses' home wouldn't give me a sick note after the abortion. I don't suppose he thought I was that close to God any more. I shouldn't have had it done on the National Health but I had to. I'd spent all the spare money I had on clothes. When I went shopping with Charlie Fox.

And there were three letters waiting for me on the kitchen table. One internal. Two external.

The internal letter said that if I didn't return to work within the next week or produce a letter of resignation, my place within the nursing school could no longer be guaranteed. Unless there was a signed doctor's letter saying exactly what was wrong with me, accompanied by a sick note, then disciplinary procedures would ensue. The letter also noted that my contributions to the nursing union had not been paid since I had not filled in the annual renewal forms. Therefore representations from any union at such a late stage would not be tolerated. They were sorry to have to deliver ultimatums but since places in nursing school were so sought after, it was not fair for the hospital to continue to resource a nurse who had not completed seventy per cent of the required course time allocated.

It was the allocated bit that got me.

The first external letter was from the police. They were very concerned that I had not answered any of their previous letters and as such were requesting, one last time, that I go to the police station before a given date, and write a full statement explaining everything that I had witnessed on the night that Kevin was thrown in the air like a rag doll. It said that Tokyo Joe was no longer on remand and had been released on bail due to there being no evidence with which to detain him.

And the second external letter told me to go back to where I came from. I was surprised they'd bothered to put a stamp on it.

There was nowhere to go. I thought about his fiancée and her horse. I would have liked a horse.

Chapter 22

Alone again. Contemplating the killing. My slaughter of the innocent. Arnie came to see me. I knew it was him. One o'clock in the morning. He came to my room. Knocked on my door. Wouldn't answer when I called out. Put a note under. Another note. Another fucking letter.

I saw the white paper inch under bit by bit. A long thin white note. Like how you make for to light the fire or the gas cooker when the pilot doesn't work. It inched under dead slow. And he wouldn't say anything. It wasn't a Get-well-quick note from Charlie. That would have been all right. I'd have liked that. But the note crawled under the door too ugly for that. That note had ugly all over it. It filled up the room with the evil black eyes of my baby. Eggy eyes in black. Slits of knowing. Under the door.

'Slow Train Coming' was still coming out of my music centre. Under the blankets I felt for where the baby should have been. I looked at my hands, my baby hands, and I wished that the biffo never said she liked them. I killed a baby and the biffo sat and cried on her bed ... no legs to run away with. My guilt brought that note to me. My debt to God was written on it. On that paper. On the floor. Down there by the door.

But I couldn't go to it. To my execution. I wasn't ready. My breathing was regular. Beating away at me. Daring me to take another breath. Daring me to stop. Daring me ever to be comfortable again. The choking matron cape on the back of the door showed me how to hang. Gave me encouragement with the note on the floor to end it all. Brown toilet cider bottles, some fallen, my audience. Lined up watching me. *But you're gonna have to serve somebody*. How did Bob Dylan know that? Know that we had to make choices like that? Why was God letting me hear it? Right then. Right at that moment. Why wasn't there anyone on table duty in the kitchen? Putting the kettle on. Polly put the kettle on.

Legs didn't bring the note. Industry was not the postman. No. It was the spirit of the baby. Baby brought it. I got out of bed and still not ready, I went to the window. Hoping for a clue. Hoping to see or feel an answer. There was blackness outside. Not one light on. Not even in the sky. Like the world had gone out on me. Like I shouldn't have been there. My elbows knocked the pills into my audio vision. Sweets. Like Tic-Tacs. Like the brown cider bottles but smaller. Ready to take. Ready. Ready now?

If I took the pills first and then read the note, then my debt was paid, whatever it said. *Oh, when the night is disappearing, Oh . . .*

I'm useless at taking tablets. It took ages. I had to break them all in half first. Any bottle would have done. Enough aspirin would have done the trick and all my pills were better than aspirin for what I wanted to do. Then I filled a cider bottle – pouring the water carefully into the bottle with my toothbrush mug. Slowly. It was like Mass, slowly

214

filling up that bottle. I thought about the water turning into wine. I needed enough water to get the tablets down me so I had to fill it to the top.

I swung the needle off the record. Scratching it all the way on purpose. Dylan wasn't gonna watch. This was me. All me. My record. I wished I'd gone out and got cider first. If I'd known it was gonna be tonight . . . That would have been better. The water was warm and the chalk from the tablets built up on the side of my tongue making me retch. I was using the water for rinsing more than swallowing so I ran out quick. I went back to the sink and filled the bottle again. It wasn't like Mass then. It was like work.

I didn't feel the drugs working. Not for ages.

I lifted each of the cider bottles in turn looking for dregs. For that wine. I found a whole half-bottle. Not the brand I normally drink. I tasted it. Flat and metallic. I drank the lot. Then I picked up the note.

I never read it by the door. I got into bed with it. Lit a fag. I read it by the fire of my match.

Josie,
You're in the clear. Tokyo Joe is dead. Died in theatre.
Car accident.
Coming back to the ward? Oh. By the way. His sister works in the kitchens.
Arnie.

I wanted to hear . . . I *believe in you, even though we be afraid*. I wanted the music to drown out the story. The never ending fucking story. I whacked the needle back on the record. Loud. Loud. And then sleep.

*   *   *

The throttle of the hose down my throat was the first thing that bugged me. The pipe filled my mouth and snaked down to the pit of my stomach bringing my life back up to me in rhythmic bursts to a bowl which was held by brown fingers, a wedding ring and dark-red nail varnish. Up the pipe came all those images. Not of my schooldays like it should be. No. The images were of men in chairs with withered legs and dribbling lips. Men that worked down the mines for ten shillings a week came surging out of the pit of my stomach to waiting hands ready to be nursed again. I saw Arnie's toothless grin and the back of his neck. I must have been thinking about where the scissors came out. Arnie was probably in ear, nose and throat having his tonsils rearranged. And then someone was shaking me . . .

'We're going to take you to the ward now. You've pulled through just fine. Try not to move too much. Stay calm.'

Which I did.

The morning fell as shattered glass across my sleep. Punishing me with its cloudy glare. Through windows, tall-arched and bare. There were the clouds. Laughing at me. A nurse I didn't know opened the door cautiously – checking to see if I was awake. I turned my body away from her. The sun peeped out of the cloud of my rationed sky.

'There's a Sister Josephine to see you.'

And then I remembered.

I could make clouds move.

A NOTE ON THE AUTHOR

Born in London, Joanna Traynor grew up in the north
of England. She trained as a nurse, then took a
degree in psychology at Plymouth Polytechnic before
moving to London. She now lives in Devon.